MAKE·BELIEVE
BALL PLAYER

Other books by Alfred Slote
Finding Buck McHenry
A Friend Like That
Hang Tough, Paul Mather
Matt Gargan's Boy
Moving In
My Trip to Alpha I
Rabbit Ears
The Trading Game

Books about Jack Jameson and Danny One
My Robot Buddy
Omega Station
The Trouble on Janus

MAKE · BELIEVE BALL PLAYER

Alfred Slote
Drawings by Tom Newsom

HarperTrophy
A Division of HarperCollinsPublishers

Library of Congress Cataloging-in-Publication Data
Slote, Alfred.
  Make-believe ball player / by Alfred Slote ; drawings by Tom
Newsom.
    p.   cm.
  Summary: Although he's not very good at baseball, ten-year-old
Henry uses his imagination to become a better ball player.
  ISBN 0-397-32285-2. — ISBN 0-397-32286-0 (lib. bdg.)
  ISBN 0-06-440425-0 (pbk.)
  [1. Baseball—Fiction. 2. Imagination—Fiction. 3. Self-
confidence—Fiction.] I. Newsom, Tom, ill. II. Title.
PZ7.S635Mak   1989   89-30598
[Fic]—dc19   CIP
                                                          AC

First Harper Trophy edition, 1992.

To Siggy and Willie,
but definitely not to Beanbelly

MAKE·BELIEVE
BALL PLAYER

1

No hitter in there, Smitty," Ted and Mike Kohn shouted from the outfield.

"Buncha bums," Rachel Dotson called in from right.

"No stick, babe," Gary Stillwell said softly from behind his glove at shortstop. Gary was the best ball player on the team next to me. I was the Sampson Park School Tigers' number-one pitcher. Gary was number two. When he pitched, I played short.

On the bench, Mr. Stillwell, Gary's dad, hollered out in his big booming voice: "You got a no-hitter, Smitty. Just pitch away, lad."

"Let 'em hit," Tony Greene said from second, and Ed Godfrey at third just kept repeating: "Smoke 'em, Smitty. Smoke 'em."

I, Henry Smith, starting pitcher for the Sampson Park Tigers, looked in to get the signal from my catcher, Casey Prince. Old Case wiggled one finger and wagged it toward the batter. That meant he was calling for an inside fastball. Joey Marshall, the Lawton School Lions' best hitter, was up. Joe, being a plate crowder, would have a hard time getting around on an inside fastball.

I pushed my glasses back. I didn't want them to fall off when I went to a full windup. I pumped, kicked, and threw inside.

Joey swung. He did not get around on it. It went off the handle of his bat. An easy pop-up right at me.

"I got it," Kevin Kline, our first baseman shouted, running toward the mound.

"Mine," I yelled. I wasn't taking any chances on someone muffing the last out of the game. The ball came down into my glove.

Cheers went up from our sideline, the subs,

parents. Lots of "Way to go, Sampson Park," "Way to go Smitty," were sounding when Mom's voice cut into the shouts of the crowd.

"Henry!"

Silence.

"Would you please stop making that noise while Mrs. Harrington is here."

"Sorry, Mom. I forgot."

It irritated me that she called my make-believe ball games noise. She was angry, because I had promised not to play when she had a customer in the house. Especially a customer like Mrs. Harrington, who was one of the richest people in Arborville.

Mrs. Harrington bought a lot of Mom's Asian folk art. Twice now my mom has gone off to Burma, Thailand, Indonesia, Malaysia, to buy folk art. She goes into little villages and buys sculpture and weavings and pottery and has it shipped back to Michigan, where she sells it to rich ladies like Mrs. Harrington.

I knew she was expecting to sell Mrs. Harrington the five-foot white wooden elephant from Thailand.

My last pitch had hit the mattress and rolled

off into the side garden. I unhooked the mattress and hauled it to the breezeway.

Through the screen door I could hear Mrs. Harrington saying, "What on earth is Henry doing, Emily?"

"Playing make-believe baseball," Mom replied. "The boy has an overheated imagination. He hangs a mattress on the garage and pretends he is all twenty players."

Mrs. Harrington laughed. "Eighteen players, Emily. Nine to a team. But how wonderful for a child to play make-believe anything in these days of television."

"It's not wonderful at all," Mom said crossly. "The sound of that ball hitting the mattress drives me crazy. I keep waiting for the next *boof*. And sometimes the *boof* doesn't come. I relax, and then . . . *boof!*"

I laughed. The reason the *boof* doesn't come in a regular rhythm is because sometimes I try to pick a runner off first or second. But there was no point explaining that to Mom.

Mom went on, "I wouldn't mind so much if Henry would be just the players, but he has to be the coaches and the parents, too. He changes his voice for that. He's only ten years old. I don't think this is normal behavior. It would be a lot more normal if he went to the park and played a real game with real children his own age."

"More normal, perhaps, but not as much fun," Mrs. Harrington said. "Now, Emily, let's talk about that elephant you've been unable to unload."

"Mrs. Harrington," Mom said with horror in her voice, "I have not offered that to anyone. In fact, I have hidden it so you could be the first to see it. I could sell the elephant at the drop of a hat."

"Nonsense. It's too big for anyone's house but mine. Secondly, you know my husband and I are crazy about large animals. Where on earth did you get it?"

"Thailand. In a little village."

"I suppose you want an arm and a leg for it."

"Mrs. Harrington, what would I do with one of your arms or legs?"

Mrs. Harrington laughed. So did I. I could listen to Mom and her customers all day long.

"Well, Emily, what *do* you want for it?"

"My husband will kill me, but I've priced it at only eight hundred dollars."

I grinned. Mom was shameless bringing Dad in like that. Dad couldn't have cared less about her business. He was a surgeon. He worked nights and days at the hospital. Her business amused him. And sometimes irritated him.

Mom used to be a nurse. But after Dad started making money as a doctor, she quit her nursing job and had kids. My sister Melissa and me. Four years ago, when I was in first grade, Mom said she was going back to school to study art.

"I refuse to stay in the house all my life."

"What's wrong with the house?" Dad had said. And then he said something that got both Mom and Melissa mad at him. He sat back and said, "Women, my dear Emily, belong in the house."

"What did you say?" Mom had asked furiously.

So Dad said it again, sitting back in his chair like a king almost. "Women, my dear Emily, belong in the house."

"Well, I don't," Mom had snapped. "I intend to buy and sell Asian folk art."

I don't think Dad thought she'd go through

with it. But she did. When Mom finished her course at the university, she arranged for a housekeeper to take care of us for two weeks. And to Dad's surprise, she arranged a trip for herself to Asia.

Melissa and I were proud of her. Not everyone's mom did something like that. Lots of doctors' wives just play tennis all day. Our mom flies to Asia! But after a while we got to be as annoyed as Dad. Because after she returned, our house started filling up with carved animals, temple posts, puppets, statues, pots, bowls, toys. We have a big house, but suddenly you could hardly move around in it.

Worse, for a while nothing sold. I thought those carved monkeys and tigers would be with us the rest of our lives. Then one day a doctor's wife bought an Indonesian puppet, and then another doctor's wife bought a tiger, and pretty soon Mom was selling things to women who were not married to doctors. The *Arborville News* even ran an article on Mom and her collection. Lots of people started calling and coming around after that.

Mom's been back to Asia again, and once more

our house is crammed with everything from tigers and monkeys to temple bells.

There's so much stuff and it's so expensive that I was forbidden to play my make-believe games inside. That happened because one day after school I was playing a make-believe game called "tooken in the end zone." It was called that by my parents because when I was about four years old I'd put on a football helmet, and holding a tiny plastic football in my hands, I'd say (according to them):

"And the ball is tooken in the end zone by Henry Smith. Smitty is cutting upfield."

After that we always called make-believe football "tooken" for short. Well, I still play tooken. And one day last year I was playing tooken for the Chicago Bears. I had received the kickoff ten yards behind the goal line in the dining room. I ran it back through the dining room, living room, den, for a touchdown, dodging tacklers everywhere. In avoiding one vicious tackle in the front hall, I ran into one of Mom's expensive Chinese vases and it broke into a zillion pieces.

Oh was there shouting and tears! Mom cried.

I cried. That night Dad, tired from seeing patients all day, looked at the broken vase and shook his head.

"Two things are wrong," he said. "There's too much stuff in the house, and Henry, you're too big to play tooken or any make-believe game indoors."

"Do you want me to rent a store, Larry?" Mom asked, knowing Dad did not want her to spend any more money on the art than she already was spending.

"No," he said. "Henry will have to play his crazy games outdoors from now on."

"They're not crazy games and I don't want to play them outside."

"Why not?" Dad said. "It's nice outdoors. There's fresh air outdoors."

"I know why he doesn't want to play outside," my sister Melissa said. She's twelve, two years older than me, and knows everything.

"Why?" Dad asked.

"He's afraid someone will see him and make fun of him. Especially when they hear him pretending to be all those people, making those funny noises."

I could have kicked her. She was right, but she didn't have to say that.

"That's a chance he'll have to take, then," Dad said. He turned to me. "No more make-believe games inside, Henry."

When Dad gave an order, that was that.

I was too chicken to play outside. So for a while I gave up my games. After school I read or watched TV. But then one day this spring I got tired of reading and I went outside.

Baseball season was going to start soon.

No one was around. No neighbors, no one. I went into the breezeway and got out an old mattress that was just sitting there. I hung it from one of the garage-door handles. Then I started pitching to it. I was pitching for the New York Mets. Even though I live in Arborville, Michigan, and like everyone root for the Detroit Tigers, in my make-believe games I always pitch for the Mets or some other National League team. That's because the American League doesn't let the pitchers hit. They have designated hitters. And in my games I often make an important hit as well as pitch.

That day I was pitching for the Mets against the

New York Yankees—it was a World Series game. I had pitched and batted and fielded for two innings before I decided to add sound. At first quiet sound, but as the game got more exciting, I played everyone. Players, coaches, managers, umpires, even the broadcasters.

Of course I would stop when a deliveryman came by or a neighbor. I'd also stop when someone drove by looking for a house number. But I didn't stop when Melissa came home, which was probably a mistake. She watched me for a minute and then shook her head.

"You know what they do with people who talk to themselves?"

"I'm not talking to myself. I'm playing a game."

"They lock them up." She marched into the house.

"No, they don't," I called after her. "They put them on the stage."

I was getting back at her. Melissa wanted to be an actress when she grew up. She was always over at Junior Theater in Sampson Park trying out for a role in some play. I thought acting was baby stuff. A curtain goes up and you start making speeches.

I liked what I did more. It was realer. Also I was beginning to like playing my make-believe ball games in the driveway. It gave me more room than the living room, dining room, kitchen, and den combined. And Mom was so glad to have me out of the house, she even let me draw a home plate on the mattress.

The only rule was: I had to quit when a customer was inside. Like Mrs. Harrington.

After I pushed the mattress back into its spot in the breezeway, I wondered what to do next. It was Saturday. A Saturday in summer can be very boring. A few birds were twittering in the trees, and a yellow butterfly was crisscrossing Mom's flowers.

I could hear some kids shouting at Sampson Park, but I sure wasn't going over there.

The side door opened, and Mom came out looking pleased.

"How is it going?" I asked.

"Mrs. Harrington is buying the elephant."

"Hooray."

"Sshh. Not so loud."

She opened the garage door.

"What're you doing?"

"I've got to find a carton big enough for it. She wants to sneak it into her house. It's to be a surprise for Mr. Harrington tonight."

"He'll sure be surprised when he finds an elephant in his living room."

"He'll be delighted," Mom said. She started tossing boxes and cartons about.

"Do you want me to help you find a carton?"

"Henry, the best thing you could do for me is to go to the park and find someone your age to play with."

"Nobody my age wants to play with me."

"How do you know that if you don't go and see? Ah, this is big enough."

She found a carton almost as big as she was.

"You can't put the elephant in that and carry it, Mom."

"Your father will help me. Now if you really want to be helpful, neaten up the mess I made and then go and play in the park. Your sister has no problem going to the park."

"She goes inside the theater."

"You can go there too."

"I'm a ball player," I said.

She went back into the house.

I stacked up the cartons. Then I waited around for Mrs. Harrington to leave so I could start playing again. Soon, though, I heard the rattle of teacups.

That was it. Mrs. Harrington was staying for tea. Now there was nothing for me to do but go to the park and hope there was nobody my age there for me to play with.

2

Sampson Park is a great park. The best park in Arborville. It's got ball diamonds, tennis courts, basketball courts, swings and teeter-totters, a wading pool that's open in summer. It has a little hill, soccer fields. And the Junior Theater building near the parking lot.

As I turned onto Baldwin Avenue, I could hear music and shouts from Junior Theater. I could also hear shouts from Diamond One, which isn't far from the theater. There's only the parking lot between them.

As I crossed the parking lot, I heard a drum go bang and someone inside the building shout: "Stand up for the king, young man."

It sounded like Melissa. I didn't hear any other actors' lines, because just then someone on Diamond One shouted: "No stick, Gary."

My heart sank. The Sampson Park Tigers, the kids from my class at Sampson Park School, were playing a game.

Maybe I should go home right now. No, they couldn't ask me to play. I hadn't signed up for this year's team. I was safe.

From the parking lot I had a good view of Diamond One. Sure enough, it was the Tigers. And player for player practically the same team that was in my make-believe game. Without me, of course.

Kevin Kline was at first, Tony Greene at second, Rachel Dotson was at short, Ed Godfrey at third. In the outfield were Mike Kohn in left, Ted Kohn, his twin brother, in center . . . and—there was no one in right field.

I should have had the sense right then and there to turn around and go home. But I wanted to watch. And I didn't think they could see me.

Gary Stillwell was pitching and Casey Prince was catching. Mr. Stillwell was on the bench. He was calling out to Ted Kohn to move more to right.

"You got to cover two fields, Ted," he boomed out.

"Hey, Mr. Stillwell, there's Henry Smith," Rachel said. "He could play right field."

Oh, Rachel.

Kevin Kline turned around. He shook his head. "Rache, we're better off with a tree than with Smith."

I made believe I didn't hear that.

"We'll have to forfeit next inning if we don't get another player," Rachel shot back.

"Time, ump," Mr. Stillwell called. He looked toward me.

Run, a little voice inside me said. Beat it. Scoot!

But I just stood there with my baseball glove. And all the while I could hear the play being rehearsed in the nearby theater.

"Your majesty, I'm here because I think I can make the princess talk."

"Nonsense, Jack," a little high-pitched voice replied, "better men than you have tried. Go home before you lose your life."

"King," said an adult voice (the director's?), "you've got to sound more kingly."

"Henry," Mr. Stillwell said, "we need a ninth

player by the second inning or we default the game. What do you say?"

"Smith'll mess up terrible, Mr. Stillwell," Ed Godfrey said. "Maybe someone else'll come along."

"No one else is gonna come along," Gary said.

The plate umpire intercepted Mr. Stillwell on his way out to me. He was about sixteen years old. "Is he in fifth grade, Coach?" he asked in a high squeaky voice.

"Yeah, he's in our class, Jimmy," Kevin said to the ump. "He was on our team two years ago."

"Henry's still on our team roster, Jim." Mr. Stillwell's voice boomed out even though he was only six feet away from the umpire.

Gary told me once his dad was a construction foreman. I guess he shouted a lot in his business.

"Henry," he shouted at me, "it's time for your comeback, lad. Get over there in right field."

The "comeback" was about how badly I'd played in third grade. I was okay in second grade, when there was no pitching. We hit off a tee then. But in third grade pitching started. And I struck out all the time.

I wasn't much better in the field. I think I caught

only one ball all season. I just don't see very well. Even with strong glasses.

In fourth grade I didn't even go out for the team. Though Mr. Stillwell told me he'd keep me on the roster in case I changed my mind. Which I didn't think I ever would.

"Come on, Henry, we need you," Casey called from behind the bat.

That settled it. If old Case wanted me to play, I would.

"Okay," I said, and tried to look brave. I hustled onto the field.

"Henry Smith's our ninth man, Dick," Mr. Stillwell informed the other coach.

The other coach laughed. "Suits me." He must have remembered me from two years ago.

I squinted to see who the other team was. They had on orange T-shirts. It looked like the Angell School Comets. They were tough.

"Batter up," said the squeaky-voiced ump named Jimmy.

I pounded my glove. I wasn't pounding it as hard as my heart was pounding me.

I took a deep breath. And then to make my

shakes go away, I shouted: "No stick in there, Gary."

Everyone else was yelling, so thank goodness no one heard me.

Gary threw two fastballs for strikes, and then the batter popped up to Kevin Kline at first. He gobbled it up.

"Way to go, Kev," I called out, thinking I probably should have moved in to back him up in case he dropped it. I really didn't have an outfielder's instincts. But right field was always where they put me. That's where the fewest balls are supposed to be hit.

The infield whipped the ball around. I wished Mom could see me now.

I felt a lot calmer when the next batter grounded out to Kevin, who made the play unassisted. Though again I probably should have moved in to back him up. But Kevin didn't miss it. It was all just like my make-believe game. Only it was Gary's fastball they weren't getting around on.

The third batter fouled out to Casey. And we were up to bat.

I ran in. Ted Kohn ran in with me. "They're

not getting around on Gary's fastball," he said.

"I know that," I said, miffed that he felt he had to point that out to me.

"That means you could be getting some business out in right field from right-handed batters swinging late."

"Right," I said, wondering if he was trying to make me nervous.

"Keep on your toes, Henry," Ted said, and slapped me on the arm with his glove. I grinned and nodded.

"All right, Sampson Park, down on the bench," Mr. Stillwell boomed out. "We're not gonna default this game, thanks to Henry, and so we're gonna win it. Right?"

"Right," we said.

"Okay. Here's our batting order. Rachel, you're up first. Take a pitch. Carter was wild last year. He'll probably be wild this year. Make him throw one strike before you start swinging. There'll be two signals from the third-base coaching box. This is the take signal."

He touched both elbows and then the peak of his cap.

"I might be giving fake signals, but that one will

be to take the next pitch. You'll always get that if the count's 3 and 0. Got it?"

"Two elbows and you touch the peak of the cap," I said. "That's take the pitch."

"For Pete's sake, Henry," Ed Godfrey said. "Why announce it to them?"

Mr. Stillwell laughed. "They're warming up. They didn't hear it. But Ed's right, Henry, it doesn't pay to talk too loudly," he said, his voice booming out.

"Yes, sir." I didn't smile. I felt good. I wished my whole family could see me now.

"Bunt is the other signal to look for. That will be when I touch both elbows and then my nose and then the peak of the cap. Any questions on the signals?"

There were none.

"Okay. Tony bats second. Gary, you're hitting in the third spot. Then Casey in cleanup. Kevin, you're number five. Mike Kohn, number six. Godfrey, seven. Ted Kohn, eight." He looked at me. "Henry, you'll be batting ninth. Have you been playing ball at all?"

"Yes, sir," I said. "I play every day."

They all looked at me, surprised. I blushed.

Dummy! Now you'll have to tell them what you do in the driveway.

But Mr. Stillwell was no fool. He could tell I was sorry I'd shot my mouth off. He didn't ask me any more questions.

"Good. Now listen up, kids. We can beat these guys if we don't beat ourselves. I'm pitching Gary for three innings, then Rachel will go two. This is only gonna be a five-inning game. Okay, Rache, get up there and make him throw at least one strike. And look for the bunt signal. You'll get it if their third baseman is playing deep."

Rachel snapped a bubble and headed for the batter's box. Mr. Stillwell headed for the third-base coaching box. Tony Greene, who was up second, slipped a doughnut over his bat and started practice swinging.

"Batter up," Jimmy the ump squeaked.

"Give it a ride," Mr. Stillwell boomed out from the third-base coaching box. This after he had privately told Rachel not to swing. That was kind of clever, I thought. I've got to remember that for my make-believe games.

Rachel stepped into the batter's box, and our bench erupted with noise.

"No pitcher, Rache."

"Picking peaches, Rache."

Their team talked it up too.

"Girls can't hit," their second baseman yelled.

"Better than you," I shouted back.

Gary Stillwell looked at me and laughed. "Thatta boy, Henry."

I wished he'd call me Smitty. "Henry" just didn't sound like a ball player. Unless you were Henry Aaron who broke Babe Ruth's record. And then he was called "Hank."

I shouted lots of stuff though. Like: "Make 'em pitch to you, Rache," "He's scared of you, Rache," "He's a humpty-dumpty, Rache." (I read that one in a sports magazine.)

Maybe I wasn't such a good athlete, but I was good with words. I get A's in school. And this was fun. Sitting on the bench again with the guys. Being part of a real team again. I was kind of glad Mrs. Harrington had come to our house. This really was better than make-believe ball.

At least it was till the top of the next inning.

3

Although Rachel worked Tom Carter, their pitcher, for a walk, we didn't get any runs that inning because Tony forced her at second for our first out. Then Gary lined out to left, and Casey flied out to center field.

As I trotted out to right field, I was thinking that Carter didn't look all that fast and maybe even I could get a piece of the ball. Or crouch and work him for a walk.

After I got on, I'd take a big lead off first and draw a wild throw and hop it to second, and all the guys and Mr. Stillwell would call out: "Way to go, Smitty."

"Batter up," the umpire squeaked, and I paid attention to the real game.

Their number-four hitter was their first baseman, Michael Phelps, and he was a lefty. Ted shifted automatically toward right field. Rachel at shortstop moved toward second, and at first base Kevin Kline instinctively moved back.

Which was silly, since the right-handed hitters were not getting around on Gary's fastball and there was no reason to think the lefties would. But everyone always automatically shifts for a left-handed hitter.

In left field, Mike Kohn shouted: "Hey, Mr. Stillwell, do you want me to switch fields with Henry?"

"No, you stay right where you are, Mike," Mr. Stillwell boomed. "Pitch away," he yelled to his son, Gary.

Which was his way of telling Gary to keep on throwing hard stuff. And Gary did. He got a quick strike on Michael Phelps, then a ball, then another ball, then a strike, then a ball . . . and then Phelps started fouling off pitches.

I thought to myself: If I were pitching, I'd take something off the fastball. The guy has good wrists, good bat control, he's setting up for the fastball. He's starting to time it.

I'd give him the big motion and then throw a change-up. On 3 and 2. He'd never expect it. He'd be way out ahead of it. He'd miss it. And Phelps did. He was way out ahead of the ball. He swung and missed it by a foot and almost fell down in the batter's box.

"Way to go, Smitty," the guys behind me yelled as they whipped the ball around the infield.

Old Case made an approving fist at me.

"That's using the old noodle, Smitty," Mr. Stillwell yelled.

"Good pitch, Smitty," Rachel called.

"Lucky," their third-base coach said.

"Henry!" Tony Greene screamed at me.

I blinked. Michael Phelps was running to first. He'd hit the ball somewhere. Kevin Kline was looking up at the sky.

"All yours, Henry," Mr. Stillwell's big voice was booming frantically.

Yes, all mine. But where was it? I stepped back, then in, then back, and then *crash*, *bam*, pain, and down I went.

I heard shouts from far away. "All the way, Mike. . . ."

I heard footsteps on the ground. Ted Kohn grunting. He was chasing the ball.

Cheers. Groans. And the earth pounded more in my ear. People were running to me. I couldn't see them. I couldn't see anyone. My head was throbbing. Everything was dark.

"Stand back, boys," Mr. Stillwell shouted. "Give Henry air."

"His glasses are broken," someone said.

"That's the least of it," someone else said.

"His father's a doctor, Mr. Stillwell."

"Henry, can you hear me? It's Mr. Stillwell. If you can hear me, open your eyes."

I opened my eyes. Mr. Stillwell's face was a blur, just inches away. Slowly, his features swam into focus. He looked scared. Beyond him I could see Jimmy the ump also looking scared, and the bases ump looking scared, and the other coach and all the kids from both teams. Everyone looked scared.

"He could have a concussion," Mike Kohn said.

"Henry, can you talk?" Mr. Stillwell yelled.

"Yes. I think so."

He looked relieved.

"Henry can always talk," Kevin Kline muttered. "That's what he was doing when Phelps hit the ball. Talking to himself. I could hear him from first base."

"I could hear him from second," Tony Greene said.

"It's my fault, Henry," Gary Stillwell said. "I threw a dumb pitch. A change-up. Phelps'd never a gotten around on a fastball."

I looked at Gary and tried to smile. I hated for Gary to feel bad. "No, I threw it too, Gary. It was the right pitch to throw."

Mr. Stillwell frowned. He thought it was a strange thing to say. He held three big fingers in front of my nose. "How many fingers am I holding up, Henry?"

"Three."

"What's the day today?"

"Saturday."

"Do you know what happened to you just now?"

"A fly ball hit me on the head."

Mr. Stillwell stood up. "I think he's all right."

"He's got a big bump on his head," someone said.

"It'll improve his looks," Ed Godfrey said.

"All right, Henry," Mr. Stillwell said, "sit up. But sit up slowly."

I sat up slowly.

"How do you feel, lad?"

"Fine."

"Woozy?"

"No, sir."

"Headache? Nausea?"

"No, sir."

"Can you stand up?"

He held his hand out, and I took it and got to my feet.

"How does that feel?"

"Okay."

"Is anyone home in your house?"

"My mother."

"I'm going to take you there right now."

"I'm all right, Mr. Stillwell. I can play."

"That's a matter of opinion," Kevin Kline said.

"Another day, Henry," Mr. Stillwell said.

"Another team, too," Ed Godfrey muttered.

"I've got to play, Mr. Stillwell. You'll default with only eight players."

"It'll be a closer game if we default," Tony Greene said.

"Let's have none of that," Mr. Stillwell growled. "Henry did his best out here."

"Here are your glasses, Henry," Rachel said. "The frame's bent."

"That's okay. Thanks, Rache."

They slid down my nose. A couple of kids laughed. I knew I looked funny.

"Here's your glove, Henry," Casey Prince said.

"Thanks, Casey."

"Ump," Mr. Stillwell said, "I guess that's the game. There's not much chance of another kid showing up now. And I don't want to take a chance with the boy's health."

"You know I don't like winning this way, Frank," the other coach said.

"I know that, Dick. I'm sorry we couldn't field a full team. Sampson Park Tigers," Mr. Stillwell's voice boomed out, "we'll stick here for some practice."

"We could play an unofficial game," the other coach said.

"That's better than nothing," Mr. Stillwell said, forcing a smile to his face.

"You'll have to do it without umps," Jimmy the ump said.

"That's all right, Jim," Mr. Stillwell boomed. "Just leave us the bases. I'll get them back to the Rec Department after the game. Henry, you still live on Colton Lane, don't ya?"

"Yes, sir, but I feel fine. I could stay and play."

"No way, lad. Not after that knock on the head. You ought to be watched. Give me five minutes to run the boy home, Dick. Let's go, Henry."

It was embarrassing . . . leaving, with everyone watching.

"So long, Henry," Rachel said.

"Take it easy, Henry," Casey said.

"You made a good try for the ball, Henry," Gary called after me. No one else said a thing.

Mr. Stillwell held on to my arm as we walked to his pickup truck.

"You mustn't feel bad about this, Henry. It can happen to the best of them. Even major leaguers get hit on the head by balls they've lost in the sun."

I stared at him. Did he really think that? Or was he offering me an excuse? I hesitated and then I shook my head. "I didn't lose it in the sun, Mr. Stillwell. I wasn't paying attention."

"Oh."

"But I might've lost it in the sun if I was paying attention."

He was startled, and then he laughed. "Henry, in baseball you've got to pay attention all the time. Even when you're not in the action. Because you could be at any second."

We turned left on Granger, crossed the intersection, and pulled up in front of our house. Mrs. Harrington's Cadillac was still in our driveway.

"Is that your Cadillac?"

"It's one of my mom's customers."

"Then I won't go in. But you tell her what happened, and that I think she and your dad ought to keep a close eye on you for the next twenty-four hours. You could have a slight concussion."

"What's a concussion, Mr. Stillwell?"

It was a word I'd used too, but I didn't exactly know what it meant.

"It's a swelling inside your head."

"I don't have that. I've got a bump on the outside."

He laughed. "Show her that then."

"I will."

As soon as Mom sees that bump, she'll never make me play real baseball again. Some good could come out of this embarrassing event.

4

Mom and Mrs. Harrington were still drinking tea. Melissa was at the table with them, reading scripts from her theater stuff. She looked at me.

"What happened to your glasses?"

All they cared about in this family were *things*.

"I got hurt." I sailed my glove over a tiger's head and onto an Asian folk-art stool.

"Henry!" Mom exclaimed. Not seeing me, just my glove sailing over her art collection.

"Where did you get hurt, Henry?" Mrs. Harrington asked.

"On my head. I have a big bump."

"That big bump is your nose," Melissa said.

"Oh, is it? Does this look like my nose?"

I bent over so she could see my forehead.

"Oh, my goodness," Mrs. Harrington said, "that is a big bump."

"I told you," I said to Melissa.

"His glasses are broken too, Mom," Melissa said. But Mom didn't care about my glasses. She even didn't care about her art collection. She was feeling the bump on my forehead.

"Ouch. That hurts."

"What happened?"

I took a deep breath. "I got into a game with my old team, the Sampson Park Tigers. I was playing second base. There was a ground ball and a runner going to second. I dove for the ball and collided with the runner. A guy named Michael Phelps. He goes to Angell School. I caught the ball and tagged him, but . . ." I shrugged.

"We better put some ice on it right away," Mom said. She'd stopped listening to me halfway through my recital.

"Well, Emily, I'll leave you to look after your wounded child. I'm sure he'll be all right. About the elephant . . ."

"Larry and I will bring it over after dinner," Mom said, going to the refrigerator and getting out a tray of ice. "Melissa, will you see Mrs. Harrington to the door?"

"Thank you, Melissa, but I'm not such an old crock that I can't see myself to the door."

"Sit down, Henry," Mom said. "Take off your glasses."

"I don't want ice."

"It will help keep the swelling down." She put about six ice cubes in a dish towel and pressed it against my forehead.

"Ouch."

"I'm not hurting you."

"Yes, you are."

"Tell us what really happened, Henry," Melissa said. "You bumped into a telephone pole, didn't you?"

"You're funny. I told you how it happened. In a baseball game."

"Here, you hold the ice, Henry."

"Where are you going?"

"To call your father. I think he ought to look at it."

"Mom, I'm all right."

But she was already calling him.

"Have no fear, brother dear, she'll never get hold of him. He's probably operating. Can you read while you hold that ice?"

"Read what?"

"The script for this play. I'm trying out for the queen in *The Princess Who Wouldn't Talk*. I need someone to feed me lines."

"Feed you lines?"

"Read the line before mine, stupid."

"You call me stupid and I won't read anything."

"Sorry. You're not stupid. Here, you be the king. I'm the queen. You start right here. 'I wonder what's ailing our daughter.' Okay?"

"You just said it. Why do you want me to say it?"

"Because it's dialogue. It's a play. And that's what will happen at the auditions on Wednesday. Someone's going to read the king while I read the queen. So I'm asking you to help me rehearse it!"

"My bump hurts."

"This will make you forget about it. Read!"

I read: *I wonder what's ailing our daughter.*

"Can't you sound more kingly?"

"I've never been a king and I don't feel so good."

"All right, read it again."

I read the line again. Just as badly.

Melissa read her lines in a phony queenly voice: *I think we have a stubborn girl on our hands. I think she enjoys being sick.*

I'm angry, I read. *No one should enjoy being sick.* The ice felt so cold. I couldn't hold it there much longer.

"Try to sound a little angry, Henry." She read: *I think we've got to send for more doctors.*

"We don't need more doctors," Mom said, coming back into the dining room. "All we need is one doctor, your father, but we can never find him. How does it feel, Henry?"

"The ice hurts more than the bump."

"Just keep holding it as long as you can. Melissa, I want you to sit here with Henry tonight after supper while your father and I take the elephant over to Mrs. Harrington's."

"I don't need a baby-sitter. I can take care of myself better than Melissa can take care of me."

"It's not just you, Henry. I have a lot of valuable things here now."

"I can call nine-one-one just as fast as she can."

"All right," Mom said. "We'll discuss it later. For all I know your father will want to take you to the hospital and get your head x-rayed."

"I don't want my head x-rayed," I said angrily.

"Now you're angry," Melissa said. "Read the line that way, Henry."

My sister has a one-track mind. I read in an angry voice: *I'm angry. No one should enjoy being sick!*

"You sound angry but not kingly."

There was no satisfying her.

Mom took the dish towel and ice from me and examined the bump.

"It doesn't look any worse," she said. "How does it feel?"

"It still hurts."

"Keep holding it."

I held the ice, and without thinking if I was supposed to or not, I read the next line in the play. It belonged to a guard.

Your Majesty, there's a young man here who says he can make the princess talk.

What's his name? I read, changing my voice from guard to king.

· 43 ·

Jack. Jack Deakins.

Well, send him in. We need help.

Okay, Jack, I read as the guard. *You can go in now.*

Thanks, I read as Jack. Changing my voice a third time: *Who do I bow to first? The king or the queen?*

"Listen to him, Mom," Melissa said, laughing. Mom was putting the teacups and saucers into the dishwasher. "He's playing everybody at once."

"Well, he's had a lot of practice playing make-believe baseball."

"At least I don't get hurt when I play make-believe baseball."

"That's true. You better stay away from the park for a while."

Finally, I thought.

Melissa read: *I like the looks of this Jack, my dear.*

I read in what I thought was a kingly voice: *He looks rather young to me.*

"That's still not very kingly," Melissa said.

I changed my voice to Jack's. *I'm not that young. My name's Jack. Jack Deakins, and I'm not afraid of anything.*

"You do Jack a lot better than the king. The trouble is we have a Jack already."

"I'm not interested in trying out for a part in your play, Mel. Do you want to rehearse or not?"

"Rehearse."

She read the queen. And I read the king, the guard, and Jack. It was kind of fun reading all those parts. Doing it, I forgot about the bump that was hurting me and the ice that was freezing me.

5

My dad is the busiest man I know. He leaves our house at six thirty A.M. every day and sometimes doesn't come back till after Melissa and I are asleep.

It's not that he doesn't love his family. He does. But he also loves his work. Curing people.

But he couldn't have had too many sick people today, because he got home for supper while we were still on dessert. We heard him come up the walk from the garage. He was whistling cheerfully.

"Sounds like he cured someone," I said.

"It's about time," Melissa said.

"I heard that," Dad said with a laugh.

Melissa ran to him and kissed him. "Mom sold the big elephant to Mrs. Harrington."

"Did you, Em?"

"I did," Mom said proudly.

Dad kissed her. "How about that?"

"And I've got a big bump on my head," I said.

"Do you?" Dad came over to me. I was still at the table. "So you do. Did you hit your little brother with some folk art, Mel?"

Melissa laughed. "No. He played in a real baseball game for a change."

"Is that right?" Dad asked, touching my bump and around it. His fingers were strong and gentle at the same time. "Well, that's what happens sometimes when you leave the world of make-believe. You bump into real life."

"I called you about it," Mom said. "But as usual, you couldn't be reached."

"Guy Cardwell came in with cardiac arrest."

"Oh dear, how is he?"

"All right for the moment." Dad's fingers kept poking around my head. "Another thing that took up some time today was your folk art collection, Em. That hurt?"

"Just a teeny bit."

"Hurt here?"

"No."

"That's good."

"What do you mean my art collection took up your time?"

"Well, I'd been wondering for some time if we shouldn't increase our homeowner's insurance policy because of it. Then after that newspaper article came out, I knew we should. How about here, Henry?" His strong and gentle fingers were now pressing on the back of my skull. "Does that hurt?"

"No," I said.

"Good." He took his hands from my head and looked into my eyes.

"What does the newspaper story have to do with increasing our insurance, Larry?"

"Burglars read newspapers, Em. Anyway, someone from the insurance company is going to call you Monday about the value of your collection. Do you have a headache, Henry?"

"No."

"Feel nauseous?"

"No."

"How about when you were back on the field? Did you feel nauseous then?"

"No. Mr. Stillwell asked me that too. He thought I might have a concussion."

"Do you think we should have him x-rayed, Larry?"

"No. I'm pretty sure he's all right. What did you get hit with, Henry?"

"A fly ball." I didn't for a second think of making up a story for Dad.

"Wait a second," Melissa said. "You told us that you collided with someone."

"Well, that happened too."

Dad laughed. "He collided with a fly ball. What's for supper, Em?"

"Chicken, and yours is cold. I'll warm it up—"

"He can't tell the truth for two straight minutes," Melissa said.

"—but you'll have to eat quickly, Larry. I promised Mrs. Harrington you'd help me carry the elephant over to her house."

"Can't, Em. Have to be back at the hospital to look at Guy Cardwell."

"Larry, this is Saturday night. Do you have to go back to the hospital tonight?"

"Yes."

"I thought Guy was Joe Gedney's patient."

"He is, but Joe's on vacation."

"Why do *you* have to cover for him?"

"Because Joe looks after my patients when we go on vacation."

"I can help you carry the elephant, Mom," Melissa said.

"I can too," I put in.

Dad spooned a chunk of grapefruit into his mouth. "I don't think carrying elephants is prescribed for a boy who got hit on the head with a fly ball. Did you lose it in the sun?"

I shook my head. Unbelievable. Dad asked the same questions Mr. Stillwell did. Mr. Stillwell could be a doctor and Dad could be a coach. Though Dad would have to develop Mr. Stillwell's booming voice. Dad's voice was more sharp. Like a knife. Well, he was a surgeon. It all fit.

"I can't leave Henry here alone, Larry. Someone probably should keep an eye on him."

"I can keep an eye on myself."

Dad looked at me. He was pleased that I was seeming to be strong and tough. "I'll be back within the hour, Em. Henry will be okay till then. Besides, Henry, you have my number at the hospital."

"Henry bent his glasses frame too," Melissa said helpfully.

"I see that," Dad said. "They're easily fixed. Were you daydreaming, Henry?"

I nodded.

"Nothing good comes out of daydreaming, son. Making up stuff is okay if you're *not* engaged in real life. If you're going to play make-believe in real life, then you better not leave the house. You'll be safe here."

He said it like a doctor. Kingly. And I believed him.

I shouldn't have.

6

I was glad when they all left: Dad to the hospital, Mom and Melissa to deliver the elephant.

I like being alone. I know you're not supposed to like being alone. You're supposed to be lonely when you're alone. But I'm not.

When I'm alone is when I can make up stuff best. It's hard to do that with people around.

I went upstairs to my room and lay down on the bed, and even though I didn't want to, I relived the awful scene on the diamond. The fly ball. Tony Greene shouting at me. And then *bam*.

I felt the bump on my forehead. It throbbed but it didn't hurt.

All in all, the Sampson Park Tigers had been pretty nice to me considering that I'd lost the game for them. Kevin Kline was right. A tree could play better in the outfield than me.

How could a tree play better than me?

I closed my eyes.

Well, for one thing, a fly ball could hit the top of a tree and then like a marble in a pinball machine drop slowly down from branch to branch. At the same time, a fast center fielder could come running over, dive, and catch the ball before it hit the ground.

Believe it or not, that's just what happened. Gary was pitching and a kid on the Angell School Comets hit a towering fly to right field. Once again we were shorthanded, playing without a right fielder. I was in center field this time. The ball hit this big oak tree and started falling down through leaves and twigs and branches. Down, down it kept dropping. Like a marble. I ran hard, never taking my eye off it. It was just about a foot above the ground when I dove and caught it in the webbing of my glove.

"Out!" yelled the ump. It was Jimmy with the high squeaky voice.

"Way to go, Smitty," Rachel yelled.

"Great catch, Smitty," Gary and Casey shouted.

Even Kevin Kline gave me a thumbs-up signal. That was the third out, and we started to run in when the other coach came charging onto the field followed by his whole team. He yelled at Jimmy the ump that the tree was out of play. That it really should be a dead ball.

Mr. Stillwell ran over and boomed out in his big voice that the tree was in play. Soon everyone was milling about under the oak tree arguing: umps, players, coaches.

"Smitty caught it fair and square," Mr. Stillwell boomed. "How can the tree be out of play when it's in fair territory? Think of the tree like the right field wall in Tiger Stadium."

"If it's like the right field wall in Tiger Stadium, Frank, then the ball's still in play." I imitated the other coach too.

"I'm changing my call," Jimmy the ump yelled. "The tree is like a wall. They're both made of wood."

That got a good laugh from everyone except Mr. Stillwell. I opened my eyes.

The phone was ringing. Darn it. What a rotten time for that to happen. I was making up a great game. It would be hard to get back to it.

I picked up the hall phone.

"Hello."

"Henry?"

"Yes."

"It's Kevin. Kevin Kline."

Kevin had never called me before in my life.

"Oh. Hi, Kevin." Why would he call me? He didn't like me at all.

His voice was friendly, though. "How're you feeling, man?"

"Okay," I said cautiously.

"Did you get a concussion?"

"No."

"Oh." He sounded a little disappointed.

"Tony's here with me. So's Ed Godfrey. Did you . . . uh . . . get a call from Mr. Stillwell?"

"No."

"Well, uh . . ." He sounded embarrassed. "He's . . . uh . . . gonna call you. Gary told us he was."

"What about?"

"He . . . uh . . . is gonna ask you to come to our game Monday."

"Really?" I couldn't believe it.

"Yeah." Kevin hesitated. "Gary says he feels bad about your getting hurt and thinks you deserve another chance. He thinks maybe if he played you in the infield, you know, maybe you'd do better."

"I don't think I would," I said.

"We don't think so either," Kevin said, relieved that I'd said it first. "That's why I'm calling you, Henry. You're still on the roster, and if you come to the game, Mr. Stillwell's got to play you for at least an inning, and . . . well, you know. . . ."

"I know. I'll make you guys lose again."

"Right. So we were thinkin' you could tell him for the good of the team that you don't want to play this year."

"I don't."

"Great. I told the guys I knew you'd understand. Well, see you around, Henry."

"See you, Kevin."

I hung up. I lay down on my bed again. I didn't feel like going back to my make-believe game.

All baseball seemed silly. I ought to go down and watch TV. Get something to eat.

The phone rang again. I let it ring and ring. It was probably going to be Mr. Stillwell. I picked it up on the sixth ring.

"Henry, this is Mr. Stillwell." His voice boomed into my ear.

"Hi, I—"

I was going to say I know why you're calling, but I never got that far.

"Henry, are you all right?" I held the receiver away from my ear. You could puncture an eardrum listening to Mr. Stillwell.

"Yes, sir."

"The phone rang and rang. Who's home with you?"

"No one. I'm okay, Mr. Stillwell. My dad examined me and said I was okay. They'll all be back soon."

"No nausea? Headaches?"

"No, sir."

"That's good. I was worried about you. So was Gary."

"Thank you. It was nice of you. I guess you had to default."

"We did. And then we played an unofficial game and beat them with eight players. It's just too bad that league rules won't let you go past the second inning with less than nine players. The default goes into the record book as a one-to-nothing loss."

"I'm sorry, Mr. Stillwell."

"Heck, Henry, it wasn't your fault. We would have had to default if you hadn't showed up. But we get another crack at them Monday. Same team. Angell School. Do you think you can make it?"

I was silent. Mr. Stillwell plunged right on. He thought I was surprised to be asked back. I would have been if Kevin hadn't called.

"I've been thinking you might do better in the infield, Henry. At second base. We could play Tony in the outfield."

Was that one of the reasons Tony was with Kevin when he called me a minute ago?

"How does that strike you, Henry?"

"Uh . . . Mr. Stillwell, I . . . uh . . . don't think I should play this year either."

"Why not, Henry?"

What a question. " 'Cause I'm no good, Mr. Stillwell."

"You won't get better by not playing."

"I can practice at home. Alone."

"It's not the same thing. It's not the same game. I've talked with Gary and Casey and Rachel, and they think you should be a sub at least."

Tears came into my eyes.

"You wouldn't start, but you could get in for an inning. Maybe two."

"Thanks, Mr. Stillwell, but I think I'd still hurt the team. If you don't have enough players and need someone so you don't forfeit, I guess I could come down, but . . ."

"I never thought of you as a quitter, Henry."

Now I really felt awful. But I'd given my word to Kevin. "Thanks, Mr. Stillwell. Thanks . . . for calling."

"I won't take your no for a final answer. You think about it, Henry. Good night, lad."

"Good night, Mr. Stillwell."

I hung up. I felt shaky. He was a nice man. Even with his booming bellowing voice. He looked like he was one of those father-coaches who had to win at all costs. But he wasn't like that at all. He was willing to have me on the team.

I lay back down on my bed. Was I doing the

right thing in saying no? Did Gary and Casey and Rachel really want me to play? Or were they just being nice?

I closed my eyes. I wished I could do something wonderful for those guys. Win a ball game for them. Suppose the rule was that you *could* play after the second inning with less than nine players.

And suppose Mr. Stillwell put me in center field.

"Henry," he said in his deep voice, "you'll have to cover right field too. Look out for that oak tree."

Which was just where I'd been in my make-believe ball game before the phone calls threw me off the track. I had just caught a ball that had fallen through the tree, and the coaches were arguing. Each of them was yelling at Jimmy the squeaky-voiced ump.

"How're you rulin' it, Jim?" Mr. Stillwell boomed out.

Jim squeaked, "I'm rulin' it a fair ball, Coach. It's like you said, Smitty caught it off the wall."

Which means, I thought, the ball's still in play and the batter's not yet out. The kid who had hit the ball was standing there under the tree arguing like everyone else. I ran over and tagged him.

"Out!" Jim stuck his thumb up.

"What do you mean, 'out'?" their coach yelled. "Time was called."

"Who called it?" Mr. Stillwell bellowed. "I didn't hear anyone call 'Time.' Quick thinking, Smitty."

Everyone pounded me on the back as we ran in for our at bat.

"Man," said Kevin Kline, "that was fast thinking."

"You're up first, Smitty," Mr. Stillwell called out. "Give it a ride."

I stepped into the batter's box.

Their pitcher made a big show out of rubbing the ball. Then he double pumped and fired. I looked that ball right into my bat. I swung and connected. Right on the nose. Shouts went up. The ball was going out. It was carrying all the way to the Junior Theater building.

Oh no, I thought, rounding first, watching the ball descend. It was going to hit a window.

There was a sharp crack of glass. Only, curiously, it seemed to come before the ball hit. And then more glass broke. And still more glass. Like little broken pieces were being pushed in. And then there was a thud and another thud. And then I came wide awake and alert.

Those noises were coming from downstairs. The breaking glass sounds had not come from a make-believe ball game. They had come from the glass door to the patio. Someone was breaking into our house.

I lay there, my eyes wide open, my heart pounding.

7

Every month the *Arborville News* runs what it calls a "crime map." It's a map that shows where burglaries or attempted burglaries have taken place the previous month. Solid blue dots stand for burglaries; blue circles stand for burglary attempts.

Mom and Dad always look at the map closely and say: "Hmm . . . none in our neighborhood." Or: "There was a burglary attempt over on Lincoln Avenue [two blocks away]. I wonder whose house it was."

And now we were going to be a solid blue dot or a blue circle.

I got up from the bed and tiptoed to the door. They had turned off the lights. A flashlight beam played around the living room. "Get that," a man whispered.

They were stealing Mom's Asian folk art.

"And that," the robber said.

I can't let them do it, I thought. My mind raced into an idea.

I bellowed out in Mr. Stillwell's voice: "Larry, there's someone down there. Get your shotgun."

Then I slammed my door and opened it again and shouted back in Dad's sharp voice: "I got it, Frank. You grab my kid's Louisville Slugger."

"I got it," Mr. Stillwell boomed.

"Then let's get 'em," Dad yelled.

I started running in place, coming down as hard as I could. I slammed my door open and shut and boomed out in Mr. Stillwell's voice: "This way, Larry!"

I was making such a racket I couldn't hear a thing from downstairs. For all I knew they were charging up the stairs right now, guns in their hands.

But then, over my racket, I heard the most beautiful sound in the world: the sound of a car

starting in our driveway. I ran to the window. A van, without lights, squealed its tires as it shot out of our driveway. It roared off down the street and passed under the streetlight. It had a white stripe in back.

I almost sank to the floor with relief. But it wasn't over yet. I ran to the hall phone and punched 911. My throat felt dry.

"Nine-one-one operator," a voice on the phone said.

Without thinking, I spoke in Dad's voice. "This is Dr. Larry Smith, Fourteen eleven Colton Lane, off Granger and Ferdon. Two burglars just broke into my house. I scared them off. They're in a van with a white stripe in the back. Driving up Hermitage Road. Without lights."

I paused. I didn't know what else to say.

"Does anyone require an ambulance?" the 911 voice asked.

"No, I'm all right," I said. And then I started to cry. Out of nowhere I cried. And in my own voice, my ten-year-old voice, I said, "I'm all right."

Silence. And then: "Sit tight, whoever you are. I'll have a police car out there right away."

I sat down on the floor. I was shaking like a leaf. I hadn't known how scared I was till I phoned 911.

It may have been all of five minutes before I heard noises outside, a car, and then flashing red lights reflected red on the walls and ceiling.

There was a banging at the front door and at the side door, and then flashlight beams played inside the dark living room, and then all the doors opened at once and there were shouts and voices and all the lights came on at once.

Looking down the stairs, I could see two policemen with guns in their hands.

"Police!" one of them shouted.

And then they both whirled about pointing their guns toward the kitchen.

"What's going on?" I heard Dad's voice. He must have just come in the side door. "I live here."

"What's your name?" a policeman asked.

"Larry Smith."

"He's the one who called in the burglary."

"I didn't call in anything. I was at the hosp— Wait a second."

Dad raced up the stairs. In a flash he was bending over me. "Henry, are you all right? What happened? Look at me, son."

"Looks like they hit him on the head," one of the policemen said.

I looked up at Dad.

"They didn't do that. Henry, are you all right?"

I nodded. I couldn't speak.

He picked me up and carried me into my room and laid me down on the bed.

"Did you see the burglars, son?" one of the cops asked.

I shook my head. Dad was quietly checking me over for bruises other than the one on my forehead.

"If you didn't call the police, mister, who did?"

The radio in the police car outside burst into sound. The second policeman ran down the stairs.

"I did," I said. Slowly the trembles were going out of me.

"Did you say you were me, Henry?"

"Yes."

I sat up.

The second cop came back up the stairs. "Car two-oh-two stopped the van on Washtenaw.

Two suspects. They're bringing them over here now."

"He didn't see them," Dad said. "He won't be able to identify them."

Dad was scared for me. He wanted to protect me.

"That's okay," the first cop said. "We'll be able to match tire tracks. Someone burned a lot of rubber leaving your driveway. Something here sure scared them."

"I did."

They stared at me.

"All right, Henry," Dad said gently, "tell us what happened."

I took a deep breath and told Dad and the two policemen everything that had happened. From after the phone call from Mr. Stillwell, and I was playing my make-believe baseball game again and had hit a home run, only it wasn't the glass in Junior Theater that broke but the glass patio door downstairs, and I realized there were burglars in the house.

"I didn't want to let them rob Mom's art, Dad."

"What did you do, Henry?"

"I pretended I was Mr. Stillwell—he's my baseball coach. He shouts a lot. I imitated him yelling at Dad to get his shotgun. And he got a baseball bat. I imitated Dad and jumped up and down and slammed the door. That's what I did."

The cops listened politely. But I could tell they didn't believe me.

Dad's face was grave. "Let's hear how you did it, Henry. How you imitated me and Mr. Stillwell. Can you stand up and do it?"

Later I thought Dad was also being a doctor. Getting me back to normal. It was the right thing to do. All the fear and shakes left me as I imitated Mr. Stillwell's booming voice and Dad's sharper one and yelled about a shotgun and a Louisville Slugger. I ran up and down and banged the door open and shut.

The policemen were flabbergasted.

But I still don't think they believed me until a third policeman came into the house.

"The tire tracks match," he called up the stairs. "We also found some loot in the van from two other burglaries in this neighborhood. One of the suspects said they left this place because there were two men in the house, and one had a shotgun and the other a baseball bat."

Silence. And then one of our policemen shook his head and said, "Well, that answers that, doesn't it?"

The other said to Dad, "You got one cool kid there, mister."

"I think so too," Dad said. He turned to me. "But why did you pretend to be me when you called nine-one-one?"

"I don't know."

"He probably thought we'd get here faster," a policeman said.

"He's right," the other said.

"*Do* you have a shotgun, Dr. Smith?" the first policeman asked.

"No," Dad said. "We don't have any guns."

"You probably don't need any with a kid like this around."

After that the policemen went outside, where a crowd of neighbors had gathered and where more police and detectives were gathered around the van with the two suspects.

I was glad I didn't have to confront the suspects. I think I would have been scared all over again. I don't know if they were told the truth then and there about the two adults, the shotgun, and the baseball bat. I was just glad they were taken away.

One of our neighbors helped Dad board up the broken patio door.

And finally, Dad and I were alone.

We looked at each other. Dad shook his head and smiled. "Henry, I owe you an apology. I'll never knock make-believe again. Especially in real life."

"I lost the game for Sampson Park because of it, Dad."

"You certainly saved us here tonight, though."

"Mom and Melissa will never believe it."

"They will when they see the broken door."

But they didn't believe it, because when they came home and Mom saw the broken patio door, she said: "Henry! You've been playing inside the house again. I told you—"

Dad laughed. "Em, Henry didn't break that door. A couple of burglars did. But one of Henry's make-believe games saved your art collection from being stolen."

"What are you talking about?"

"Tell them, Henry. Tell them what happened."

I told them.

"I don't believe it," Melissa said. "I think Henry

made all that up because he broke the door. And maybe you were playing make-believe baseball or football with him, Dad."

Aren't big sisters tough?

"Is it true, Larry?" Mom asked Dad.

"Yes. We've had a busy time here tonight. And, I suspect, it will be even busier tomorrow."

I didn't know what Dad meant by that until the next day, when the phone rang and rang and people kept coming over to our house. I think all of Arborville came over.

Including the Sampson Park Tigers and Mr. Stillwell.

8

The *Arborville News* is an afternoon paper, but on Sundays it comes out in the morning. It gets delivered to our house about eight o'clock, but we don't usually look at it till about eleven.

But that Sunday morning we were awakened early by the phone ringing and people calling to tell us what they had just read.

"Go down and get the paper, Henry," Dad said after the third phone call.

I went downstairs, and there the story was. On the front page, no less.

TEN-YEAR-OLD THWARTS
BURGLARS

Henry Smith of 1411 Colton Lane prevented a sure robbery at his house last night
by outwitting a pair of intruders, according
to chief of detectives Ron Keller.

"Dad," I yelled, "we *are* in the newspaper."

Mom, Dad, and Melissa came running down,
and Dad read the story out loud. It told how I
imitated him and "coach Frank Stillwell of the
Sampson Park Tigers in the Arborville Ten-Year-
Old Baseball League. In addition to his acting
abilities, Henry Smith plays keen baseball for the
Sampson Park Tigers."

"Oh, no, they'll think I told that to the police.
I never said I was a good baseball player."

"That's a newspaper for you," Dad said. "Making a better story out of a good one."

Mom read the account again. And when she
was done, she got scared. She dropped the paper
and hugged me. "Henry," she said.

Melissa also read it by herself. "Well," she said
when she was done, "I guess he's going to be
famous now."

The phone rang. This time it was Mrs. Harrington.

"We're all right, Mrs. Harrington," Mom said. "No, they didn't get anything. Henry saved the whole collection. . . . Did he?"

Mom came back and reported that Mr. Harrington liked the elephant just as much in the daytime as he did at night. "And he and Mrs. Harrington both think Henry ought to get a medal from the president."

The phone rang again.

"How long is this going to go on?" Melissa said.

This time it was a doctor friend of Dad's. After that it was a friend of Mom's. Then two operating-room nurses called Dad to say they'd just read the paper. Then a patient of Dad's. The last straw for Melissa was when her friends started calling and asked her to get my autograph for them.

"They want his autograph," she said. "My little brother's."

"Well, your little brother is a hero," Dad said.

"I don't care. It's tiresome."

"I think we ought to leave the phone off the hook for a while," Mom said.

"Can't do that," Dad said. "I'm on call this weekend."

It wouldn't have made any difference, because right about then the doorbell started ringing. It was neighbors wanting to know where the break-in had occurred and wanting to shake my hand.

Then we got a phone call from Channel 2 in Detroit. They wanted to send a film crew over here to interview me this morning.

"No way," Dad said. "He's too young. No interviews."

The doorbell rang while Dad was arguing with the Detroit TV station.

"It's for Henry again," Melissa called.

This time it was Mr. Stillwell and the whole Sampson Park team. They were standing on our front steps. Their bikes were all over the lawn. Mr. Stillwell's pickup truck was parked out front.

Oh, boy, I thought, they're mad at me because the newspaper story said I was a keen ball player.

"Mr. Stillwell, I didn't talk to a newspaper. I just talked to the police. And I never said I was a good ball player. I just said I . . . uh . . . imitated my baseball coach."

I felt my ears burning. It's one thing to tell your father and two policemen you imitated a baseball coach; it's another thing to say it right to the coach's face.

"Nothing to be sorry about, Henry," Mr. Stillwell boomed out. He was grinning from ear to ear. "I can always use the ink. We came over to tell you that now you've *got* to play for us tomorrow."

I stared at him.

"I got a phone call this morning from Channel Seven in Detroit. They want to take pictures of you playing in a game. So Henry, you're *starting* for us tomorrow at second base. Tony's gonna play in the outfield. The whole team's excited and happy, aren't you, gang?"

If I could have taken a picture of the whole team being excited and happy, it would have won a prize. I mean: Only Rachel and Gary and Casey looked halfway happy. And they also looked halfway worried.

But Rachel winked at me and said, "Darn right, Henry."

Kevin Kline wouldn't look at me. Ed Godfrey was staring at his sneakers. Tony Greene, whose position I was taking, stood there with his arms folded. The Kohn twins looked at the sky.

Mr. Stillwell's big voice boomed. "Tomorrow there'll be media at our game." He said "media" like it was candy. He rolled it off his tongue. "We're gonna show the whole world what classy baseball is played in the Arborville Ten-Year-Old League. Right, gang?"

"Darn right," Rachel said again.

"Can't they film a practice, Mr. Stillwell?" Kevin asked.

"They want to film a game. And I told them we've got a game tomorrow." He looked back at me. "There'll be a lot of pressure on you, Henry, but nothing you can't handle. *Two* robbers you chased off. Heck, one would've scared me to death. We'll see you at Diamond One at the park at five thirty. Right?"

I gulped. And nodded. Dad came to the door to see what was going on. When he and Mr. Stillwell saw each other, they both broke into laughter.

"Well, Dr. Smith, I see Henry got you some ink too."

"Didn't he?" Dad laughed and put his arm around me.

"Your boy's a bona fide hero," Mr. Stillwell boomed. "I'm starting him at second base tomorrow night. I hope you and Mrs. Smith can come. There's gonna be a TV crew from Channel Seven filming the game."

Dad looked at me. "That'll be a lot of pressure for you, Henry."

"Dad says Smitty can handle it," Gary said.

I almost jumped out of my skin. It was the first time anyone besides me in my make-believe games had called me that.

It had sounded so natural.

"Were you scared last night, Henry?" Rachel asked.

I nodded. I guess I'd have to earn "Smitty" from the rest of them. On the field.

"Boy, you really thought fast," Casey said, grinning. "I couldn't a done it."

"Just do the same thing on the diamond, Henry," Mr. Stillwell boomed.

"You got to run, hit, and field on the diamond, not think," Kevin muttered.

"You can think in baseball too, Kevin," Mr.

Stillwell said. "Well, congratulations, Henry. And we'll see you tomorrow at five thirty."

"So long, Henry."

"Good going, Henry."

"Way to go, Henry."

They left. Dad looked at me. "That was very nice, their coming over like that."

Melissa, who had heard the whole thing, grinned at me. "Gee, Henry. Not only do you have to play real baseball now, but you've got to do it in front of millions of people. You better not get hit by a fly ball tomorrow."

"Don't tease him, Mel," Dad said. "Henry did a wonderful thing last night."

Melissa came over and gave me a hug. "I know you did. I think you were really brave, Henry. I'm proud of you too."

"Yeah, but you're right, Mel. I better not get hit by a fly ball tomorrow."

There were more phone calls, and more people came to congratulate me, but already I was beginning to worry about tomorrow. If last night had been a nightmare, tomorrow on Diamond One could be even worse.

9

Dad hit ground balls to me that afternoon in our backyard, and I fielded most of them. But I knew it would be different in a game situation.

That night I hardly slept. For one thing, the phone was still ringing. At one point a radio station in California called wanting a phone interview with me. Someone called to tell us I'd made the Associated Press wire services. All the newspapers in the country might be running the story.

The next morning reporters from the *Arborville News* and the Detroit papers came to the house. Melissa snuck me out the back door while Mom told the reporters there would be no interviews.

"Go to the police. They have all the facts," Mom told them.

While the reporters were in front talking to Mom, I got my bike out of the garage and biked out of our backyard and down to the river. I sat by the river for a long time trying to empty out my mind. But instead of getting calmer, I was becoming more nervous. If this was what being famous was like, it was a terrible thing.

I began to feel sorry for ball players like Wade Boggs and Dwight Gooden and Kirk Gibson.

When I got back, the house was empty except for Mom. Melissa was at Junior Theater. Around three o'clock Dad called to ask how I was feeling.

"Terrible," I said.

He laughed. "You'll do fine. Just concentrate. And don't play make-believe baseball while you're playing real ball."

"I know. I know."

"I'm going to do my best to make it to the game."

"Don't come. I'll feel better if you don't come." Dad laughed.

I said the same thing to Mom.

"Nonsense," Mom said. "Of course I'll be there. I think everyone in Arborville will be there."

"What for? To see two ten-year-old teams play baseball?"

"No. They think they might be on TV."

Mom was right. The area around Diamond One was already crowded when I got there. People were sitting all over, on blankets, on chairs. There's a little bleacher that seats about forty people. There wasn't an inch of space left on it.

A white van that said Channel 7 on it was parked alongside the stands. There were TV people laying out cables, setting up lights, a microphone; a woman with a big video camera was looking at the crowd; a man carrying a battery pack was talking with people in the stands.

"Here comes our star," someone called out.

Everyone looked at me. I wished there were a hole I could have crawled into. The camera was pointed at me.

"Over here, Henry," Mr. Stillwell's voice boomed out over the others.

He was talking to a man in a white suit.

"Henry, I want you to meet Mr. Arneson, pres-

ident of the Arborville Recreational Baseball Leagues. Arne, this is Henry Smith."

Mr. Arneson had deep-blue eyes. He stuck out his hand. "Proud to meet you, Henry. You're bringing the Arborville Recreational Baseball Leagues to the attention of the world."

My knees started to shake.

"Henry, you better throw a ball around," Mr. Stillwell said, winking at me.

The Sampson Park Tigers were loosening up along the left-field foul line. To get there I had to run around the diamond, on which the Angell School Comets were having infield practice.

"There goes Henry Smith, hero," their short-stop said.

"Where's your SWAT team, Henry?" their catcher said to me.

They laughed. I ignored them.

I ran up the left-field foul line past the two umps. They were anchoring third base. One of them was our old friend Jimmy the ump.

Jimmy looked up. "Hey, congratulations, Henry," he said.

"Thanks," I said. I think he meant that.

Finally, I got to where my team was loosening up. Rachel tossed a ball at me.

"Throw easy, Henry," she said.

Throwing was probably the thing in baseball I did best. That was because of the hours I spent firing a baseball at the mattress.

"How're ya feelin', Henry?" Casey asked. He and Gary were paired off playing catch.

"Good, Casey." Why couldn't I call him "Case" the way the other kids did and the way I did in make-believe games?

"You a little scared, Henry?" Rachel asked as she tossed me one sidearm.

"A lot."

"I am too."

"I don't believe that, Rache."

"I almost threw up this afternoon."

"I hope I get a hit. I never been on TV before," Ed Godfrey said.

"They won't be taking your picture, Godfrey," Ted Kohn said.

"Yeah, it'd break the camera," Mike Kohn said.

"Funny, man."

"How many people you think are here, Case?" Gary asked.

"Lots."

"They filled the seats a half hour ago."

"That ain't so hard to do."

"Look at those girls walking back and forth in front of the camera."

"That's one way to get on TV."

"The other way's to capture two robbers."

"I didn't capture them."

"You helped, man."

"Hey, Henry, you think you'll be a cop when you grow up?"

"No."

"Here comes Ray Harvey."

Ray Harvey was on the Channel 7 news each night.

"He looks thinner than he does on TV."

"TV makes you fat, my dad says."

"Henry, he wants to interview you."

"I bet."

"He's been asking for you ever since they got here."

Ray Harvey was smiling and waving at people who were calling out his name. He came over to us.

"Which one of you is Henry?"

"Henry who?" Casey asked innocently.

Ray Harvey laughed. "C'mon. Henry Smith."

"Him," Rachel said, pointing to me.

Ray Harvey gave me an easy smile. "Henry, I'd like to ask you a few questions over by home plate, where we've got a nice background."

"No way, Ray," boomed Mr. Stillwell, coming up and taking Mr. Harvey by the arm as though they were old friends. "The lad's getting ready for a big game. But here's someone who'll give you a great interview."

Mr. Arneson stuck out his hand. "Arne Arneson. League director." He started steering the TV anchorman toward the camera behind the backstop. "Ray, I'd love to tell Channel Seven's audience about our program here in Arborville. We feel we have one of the strongest kids' baseball programs in the state."

"But—" Ray Harvey protested as he was steered away from us.

Mr. Stillwell laughed. "That's the way to throw, Henry. Nice and easy."

"I bet Henry could pitch, Mr. Stillwell," Rachel said.

"He might at that," Mr. Stillwell agreed, "but not tonight."

"I only pitch to mattresses," I said.

"Mr. Stillwell," said a high squeaky voice. Jim had come up. "Your team can take the field now."

"Thanks, Jim.

"Okay, Tigers. Gather 'round. Outfield, Gary'll hit to you. I'll hit to the infield. Ed, you're on third. Rachel short. Henry's at second. Henry, if you don't catch it cleanly, just keep it in front of you. You've got a short throw to first. Kevin, you're at first. No errors. Everyone concentrates. First catch it. *Then* throw it. Okay, kids, take the field."

"Let's go," Rachel yelled.

I felt shaky as I ran out to second base. I hoped I wouldn't trip crossing the third-base line. I didn't.

There was a lot of clapping. And I saw the TV camerawoman aim the camera at me.

"That's him," a woman said. "The kid who caught the burglars."

Now everyone was saying I'd caught them. Pretty soon it would turn out I'd tracked them down. And the truth was I hadn't even seen them.

"Play for one," Mr. Stillwell shouted.

He hit easy grounders to each of us. When my turn came, I uttered a little prayer. Please let me catch it cleanly. This is important. I've got to get off to a good start.

The crowd was silent. It was only infield practice, but everyone was watching me, including the camera. Mr. Stillwell hit me an easy grounder. I caught it and flipped it to first and breathed out.

So did everyone else on the team.

Five minutes later the game began, and in the first inning the TV crew got all the pictures they wanted and then some.

10

The Angell School Comets were up first. Gary looked nervous on the mound. He was throwing weird. Slow. Babying the ball up there. Gary threw the hardest of anyone in the ten-year-old league in Arborville.

He walked their first batter on four straight slow pitches. He threw a nice slow fat pitch to the second batter, and the guy promptly banged it into left field for a single. The runner on first stopped at second. Two men on. No one out.

Mr. Stillwell bellowed: "Gary. Don't do that. Fire away."

When Mr. Stillwell said, "Don't do that," I suddenly realized what Gary was doing. He was throwing slow pitches because he wanted them to get around on the ball and hit it to the left side . . . away from me. And it just wasn't a natural way for him to pitch.

I was embarrassed, but I didn't think anyone but me and Mr. Stillwell and Gary knew what he was doing.

Anyway, Gary started firing. He threw bullets and he threw them for strikes. He struck out their third batter on three straight pitches.

And we started hollering.

"They got holes in their bats," Rachel yelled.

"They can't see you on a Sunday," Ed Godfrey said. I didn't get that at all.

"Give 'em smoke," Kevin kept repeating. "Give 'em smoke."

Old Case behind the plate made an encouraging fist.

I didn't say anything. My throat felt dry. I didn't feel I could talk at all. The TV camera was aimed at me. They were waiting for a ball to be hit at me, and with Gary throwing bullets, someone swinging late from the right side was sure to do it.

I held my breath. The fourth batter swinging late hit a ground ball just foul past first base. Then he hit a pop-up to the right side.

"Get it," Ray Harvey shouted.

For a second I thought he was talking to me. Maybe he was. The ball was coming down between me and Kevin. I could see it but I wasn't sure I could catch it.

Kevin called me off. "I got it," he yelled, and gobbled it up.

"For Pete's sake," I heard Ray Harvey say.

I ran to second in case the runner had any ideas.

"Infield fly rule," Jimmy the ump called out. "Batter's out anyway."

Sure. I forgot about that. Someone giggled. That made it two outs. Gary looked at me worriedly. They were hitting his fastball and hitting it toward me.

"Time, ump," Rachel said, and ran into the mound. I ran in too. So did Ed and Kevin.

"Let's try a pickoff play," Rachel said. "The runner on second's taking a big lead. He's watching me, but he's not looking at Henry at all. He

· 95 ·

doesn't think Henry could catch a throw from you, Gary."

"I couldn't."

"Don't be silly. It's just like playing catch with me."

"Gary'll throw harder."

"No, I won't, Henry," Gary said.

"If you don't throw harder, you won't get him," Kevin said.

"C'mon, kids," Jimmy squeaked, "let's get the game moving. A lot of spectators are getting restless."

"We're setting up a play, ump," Rachel said.

"Listen, Henry," Gary said, "when I go to my stretch position, count one potato two and run to the bag. The ball will be there nice and easy and we'll get the guy."

"Okay," I said, though I didn't believe it.

The big crowd was getting impatient. So was Mr. Stillwell. He didn't know what was going on.

"Batter up," the plate umpire shouted.

Jimmy took his field umpiring position behind second.

Gary stepped on the rubber. He went to a

stretch position. "One potato two," I said, and cut to the bag.

"Get it," Ray Harvey called.

Gary whirled and threw. He threw a nice, easy ball. A baby could have caught it; a turtle could have outrun it. Grinning, the base runner trotted back to the bag.

I caught the ball and tagged him anyway. He laughed at me.

I said without thinking, "Out," and I said it in Jimmy's squeaky voice.

The runner turned around and yelled, "What do you mean 'out'?"

He left the bag. I tagged him again.

"*Now* you're out," Jimmy squeaked, a big grin on his face. His thumb shot upward.

For a moment no one knew what had happened except me and Jimmy. The base runner didn't even know. Their coach came out to ask what was going on.

Then Rachel got it. She chortled. She smacked me on the back. "Way to go, Henry."

She told everyone what I'd done.

Gary laughed. Casey hugged me. Tony Greene

came running in from right field and jumped on my shoulders. Kevin Kline high fived me. "That's heads-up baseball, Smitty."

I looked at him. He'd called me "Smitty."

I smiled. "No, Kev, it wasn't heads-up baseball. It was make-believe baseball."

"C'mon, Tigers, hustle in," Mr. Stillwell boomed. "The game's not over."

11

Well, my story ends here. We won the game 3–1. And I'd like to tell you I hit a home run or took part in a double play, but I didn't.

That crazy pickoff play did help take the pressure off everyone. After that play, the TV people left. They had gotten exactly what they wanted: me in action putting a tag on a runner.

We watched it that night on the news. Ray Harvey did a smooth voice-over narration. On camera, he tied it in with the robbery.

That robbery. . . . It felt as though it had happened a long time ago.

Dad never made it from the hospital to the game. Mom and Melissa gave him a blow-by-blow description. And I was so into the game, I never knew that they were there or that Dad wasn't.

After we watched the pickoff play on the news, Dad said, "Henry, it wasn't a baseball play, not really."

"I know. I didn't even do it on purpose."

"That's all to the good," Dad said. "But it does lead me to conclude that if you don't make it to the big leagues, you might have a future on Broadway."

"Speaking of which," Melissa said, "Henry, would you try out for the king in *The Princess Who Wouldn't Talk*? We haven't cast a king yet. And I think you could do it."

"Mel, I can't sound like a king. I read it the other night and you *said* I didn't sound kingly."

"That's because you don't know what a king sounds like."

"What does a king sound like?"

"Your father," Mom said, amused. "Try sounding like him."

"Now wait a second," Dad said.

"Women, my dear Emily," Mom said, "belong in the house."

I repeated it, but in Dad's voice.

"Perfect," Melissa said.

Dad shook his head. "I'm sorry I ever suggested the theater as a career for you, Henry."

I wasn't, though. On Wednesday I tried out for the part of the king and got it. Using Dad's voice all the way. Acting, it turned out, was a lot of fun. Of course I'd always been doing it. I just never thought of it as acting. Just playing make-believe.

The funny part was that now, between Junior Theater and the Sampson Park School Tigers, summer was flying by and I had no time for make-believe baseball.

But as I warned Mom, come football season, I was going to play tooken in the end zone.

"Not in the house, you won't," Mom said. "And if you have to do it outside, away from my flowers, please."

Everything had changed and nothing had changed. Mom was still dead set against make-believe ball games. That's what I thought. I was wrong.

One crisp fall afternoon I played tooken outside. I gathered in a football in the end zone next to the garage and began running it back, dodging eleven New York Giants' tackles.

The crowd rose to its feet as I faked two tacklers right into the ground. I was up to the 30-yard line already.

"All the way," they screamed.

My teammates were cheering me on from the sidelines. I leaped over one tackler and cut around another.

I crossed the 50 still going strong. Down to the 40. I raced along the sidelines. The 30 . . . the 25. . . . Only one man stood between me and the goal line, but he was their surest tackler. An all-pro.

He angled toward me. I gave him a piece of my right leg and then took it away as he dove for it. I accelerated, and with the cries of the crowd, the TV and radio announcers, my coach and teammates, ringing in my ears, I crossed the goal line. A 105-yard kickoff return!

"Touchdown!" the TV announcer yelled into his microphone.

"Touchdown!" the fans screamed.

And then a familiar voice split the air.

"Way to go, Smitty!"

It was Mom. She had both arms in the air, signaling touchdown. I laughed. And then I spiked the ball . . . away from her flowers.

YA
Fic   Early Sorrow.
Ear

        212p.   14.95 5/94

EARLY SORROW

Ten Stories of Youth

SELECTED BY

Charlotte Zolotow

An Ursula Nordstrom Book

HarperCollins*Publishers*

Once again I want to thank Harper & Row,
specifically Mike Bessie, Win Knowlton, and
Brooks Thomas, for the Cass Canfield Sabbatical
Award, which allowed me to complete this collection.

Designed by Harriett Barton
4   5   6   7   8   9   10

Library of Congress Cataloging-in-Publication Data
Early sorrow.
  "An Ursula Nordstrom book."
  Contents: Michael Egerton / by Reynolds Price—
The Visitor / by Elizabeth Bowen—Short Papa / by
James Purdy—[etc.]
  1. Short stories, American.   2. Short stories, English.
[1. Short stories]   1. Zolotow, Charlotte, 1915—
PZ5.E26   1986   [Fic]   79-2669
ISBN 0-06-026936-7
ISBN 0-06-026937-5 (lib. bdg.)

*For Bill Morris, to whose knowledge
and appreciation of children's literature
so many of us are deeply indebted.*

Contents

Introduction

Sorrow takes many forms and comes in many ways. When we feel it in youth, that time of terrible intensity, it can be compounded by the confusion of outside influences, and carry forward into the kind of adults we become.

This is a collection of ten stories about early sorrow. Each is rich and compelling on its own; each is totally different from the others. Written in contrasting voices and styles, by such various authors as Carson Mc-Cullers and Katherine Mansfield, from such disparate times as E. L. Doctorow's and Stephen Vincent Benét's, they are gathered here by their common theme.

Some of these stories are about love. Some are about loss through divorce, separation, or death. It is my hope that they will awaken in both older and younger readers a compassion for one another, and remind us that we are more united than separated by differences in age, since time makes all life flow together.

Charlotte Zolotow

NINA

H. E. Bates

When first the visitor came to call on them it was spring. For tea there were cream pies, and cakes with cinnamon; and about the room were set pots of anemones, primroses and blackthorn Nina had gathered from the woods the previous day. The sun was shining; and all through tea the visitor sat as if transfigured, his high forehead, his black hair, and the shoulders of his jacket fringed with lines of a feathery gold.

But to Nina it also seemed that after shaking hands with her, and giving her one hasty, half-shy look and asking her name, he did not notice her again. Between him and her mother began a long conversation on all sorts of subjects, on music, the spring, the early heat, the different Easter customs in different countries, with a mention of her father, who had died a year before.

And from this conversation she gathered that Strawn, the visitor, was a pianist and had lived abroad, but that when she had been a little girl had lived in

3

England and visited them often, a friend of her father's. She could not remember this, but the thought
that he played on the piano thrilled her. She began to
say to herself, regarding shyly his long, white fingers,
his sunny face and dark eyes:

"After tea I will ask if he will play to us and perhaps
hear me play."

For a long time she sat still, wondering in a shy,
apprehensive way what he would think of her.

All the time her mother and the visitor would talk
absorbedly to each other. Outside a soft wind was
blowing: emerald buds bounced against each other
and dust sometimes came tinkling up against the panes.
The edges of some pines at the end of the road were
being turned first gold, then red, by the setting sun
and among them were already masses of darkness.
Tea went on for a long time until the lines of gold
vanished from Strawn's face and all the colours of the
room merged into one colour.

Nevertheless, all this time, she thought: "In a little
while he will say something to me. Soon he will ask
if I play."

And she began to think of what she should play to
him, a dance of Brahms', some Schumann, some
Mozart. She lost herself in dreaming of this, lost herself so completely that when she suddenly looked up
and saw him laughing, the reality of the laugh, the

4

sparkle of his eyes and the joyful way he smacked his hands together came as a shock to her.

Just at that moment he looked at her too. She flushed a dark crimson and began tapping her nails together in confusion. Then she waited for him to speak to her and in the midst of her bewilderment was filled suddenly with a desire to know him better, to attract and impress him.

When he did not speak to her she thought with disappointment and sadness, "It's because I'm only a girl, only seventeen."

And from that moment she had a constant longing: "If only I were older, only a little older!"

Soon afterwards, at last, tea was finished. Nina's mother and the visitor got up, still talking, and went into the garden. Nina remained behind and for a long time sat watching with a dreamy, naive expression the chair where Strawn had sat. Each time she thought of his silence towards her she felt hurt, envious of her mother, disappointed and sad.

Before, she had been irresponsible and vivacious, playing in the woods, the garden and on the piano without care. Now, each time she thought of the visitor, she was conscious of a desire to be attractive, but what precise degree of attraction would be best, if she should be smiling, graceful, quiet or melancholy, she did not know.

She got up and looked at her face in the glass. In appearance she was dark, with a skin which in the twilight was pale, waxen and alight. And that she should be able to use this loveliness, together with that of her voice, her movements and her playing, in order to attract anyone, thrilled her excitedly.

Soon afterwards she opened the window an inch or two, and sitting down at the piano began playing. And while playing she thought of her mother and Strawn walking under the cherry trees, among the raspberry and gooseberry bushes, and all the time hoped and wondered if they would hear her.

And then, sometime later, she heard voices, footsteps and Strawn saying, "Good-bye."

And soon afterwards she was conscious of shaking hands, waiting for Strawn to say something about the piece she had played with the window open and of an acute, lingering disappointment because he said nothing, scarcely even looked at her, but walked abruptly away. . . .

Some time later she learned that he had moved his residence and in future would be nearer them and come to see them and even stay more often.

She played the piano untiringly and before each visit contrived somehow to decorate everywhere with spring flowers, arrange her hair attractively, and make the special cream pies which she believed he loved.

But at each visit it seemed to her that he gave his attention only to her mother. And each time he left she was wretched, angry, disappointed and sad.

Then it happened that once when he came, unexpected, her mother was not there. It was evening time and Nina was among the gooseberry bushes at the bottom of the garden, eating young gooseberries and thinking how thrilling it would be if Strawn were to come suddenly and find her there.

When his head appeared among the trees and he called: "Where are you?" she was startled and scratched her hands and dropped some gooseberries she had been holding in her dress.

After that she did not move, but only watched him come towards her. As he came to her he half-smiled and said:

"It's Nina, isn't it?"

She nodded and said: "My mother isn't here."

"She didn't know, she was not expecting me," he smiled. He took off his hat and fanned his face and blew out his cheeks like a boy. She laughed shyly and said:

"Perhaps you had better come and sit down and wait for her. She's gone to the village."

He seemed not to hear this and asked: "What are you eating?"

"Gooseberries."

"I'll eat some too," he said.

And for a long time afterwards she remembered the way he foraged in the bushes, picking gooseberries; and how, throwing them up in the air he caught them again in his mouth, crunched them up at once and made sour faces. And all the time, as she watched him and laughed, it seemed that the past was only a dream and that her emotions about him were at last what she had wished them to be, and were fierce and passionate, like little revolutions in the streets of her mind.

"I can talk and be understood!" she thought.

They fell into conversation and soon afterwards left off picking gooseberries and went and sat in the summerhouse and talked of the spring. Later they talked of herself and of music. The way he talked she thought wonderful and enchanting. And while listening to him she clasped her hands and let her face fall sideways upon them, lightly and with joy.

Once she unclasped her hands, looked serious and said:

"I want to ask you something."

"What is it you want to ask?"

And she said timidly: "Why is it you haven't spoken to me?"

For having spoken she felt bewildered and ashamed.

8

She tried to turn away, but he seized her hands and tried to look into her hot, flushed face, which she hung downwards to her breast. And he began to whisper:

"Nina, tell me what I've done, forgive me, you don't understand."

But suddenly she had no thought of sadness and was aware only of the superb happiness given her by his voice and his presence.

"I only wanted to talk to you!" she cried.

He laughed. Nina laughed too and said:

"But now all that's gone—it's all right. I'm happy!"

They went on talking. Dusk fell, the little gooseberries lost themselves in the dark trees, and above the bigger trees spread like broad, black umbrellas put up to keep off the dew. The dusk, the warm-smelling silence and Strawn's voice excited her imagination. She began to tell herself, with little flutters of joy, "He is in love with me, he is in love with me!"

She thought that she too was in love. And from that moment it seemed that her love was serious, passionate and tender. As they sat there Strawn saw that she had scratched her hands and, wetting his handkerchief, bathed off the blood. And it seemed to Nina that now where the smart had been burned something joyful and pleasant instead.

As they went into the house to look for her mother

she kept laughing. Her eyes would light up and she would exclaim:

"I'm so happy—and yet I don't know why!"

"Yes? That's lovely," he would say.

She would watch if he were watching her. And all the time it seemed to her that he must know why she was so happy, why she kept saying absurd things, flinging her arms about, and asking him to look at the trees, the sky and the flowers sleeping in the painted stillness of coming darkness.

When he did not seem to notice the reason of all this she would console herself: "It will happen! It will come!"

Now she no longer wanted to play to him or hear him play, but only to be near him, to be excited by him and listen to his voice.

She would look at his face and think joyfully: "He understands!"

At the sight of her mother, who came suddenly running down the steps of the house saying, "I'm sorry, I'm sorry!" she was no longer envious or sad. When they all three went into the house and Strawn for the first time played Mozart on the piano to them, little thrills of pure joy like lovely scales ran up and down her spine, and when he ceased playing, apologized and declared, "I'm getting old," she thought of the way he had blown his cheeks out like a boy and eaten gooseberries in the garden. And she thought of him only as being young, understanding and splendid.

When she went to bed at last he smiled and pressed her hand and said: "Have nice dreams."

On the stairs and in her bedroom, where she did not undress but sat at the window listening to the owls, she thought of this, of his splendid, dark eyes, his voice, of the entrancing, wonderful things he had said. And she thought that she loved him and perhaps was loved, and was conscious of looking forward to summer and of what summer would be like with him.

It seemed that long afterwards, as she still sat there, she heard the voices of Strawn and her mother coming from below.

Her heart raced, her body trembled and suddenly she longed to go down and look at him for one moment longer.

She took off her shoes and went down. On the stairs and everywhere it was dark, and the darkness seemed to give Strawn's voice a new sound of enchantment and mystery.

At the foot of the stairs she stood still and listened and heard him say:

"Sometimes it's a thousand, sometimes only five hundred."

Nina went forward, stood at the open door of the

drawing room and, after listening a moment, looked in. And she saw suddenly that in a sad sort of way, before the fire, her mother was pressing her temples against Strawn's knees and that every now and then she would look up, murmur something and make passionate little signs on his knees, and that Strawn would bend down, whisper in return and draw away his face with tenderness and longing.

She started. Beginning to breathe heavily she did not know what to do with the immense sadness which filled her.

But in a little while she turned, retreated slowly upstairs and in a dull, stupefied way, undressed and got into bed. And as she lay there looking at the stars she began to cry, and it seemed to her that the sounds she made turned and went suddenly through her head, like tiresome children playing up and down stairs. And it seemed too that the scratches on her hands began to smart again and that in her mouth returned a taste of something unpleasant and sour, like the taste of young gooseberries.

MICHAEL EGERTON

Reynolds Price

He was the first boy I met at camp. He had got there before me, and he and a man were taking things out of a suitcase when I walked into the cabin. He came over and started talking right away without even knowing me. He even shook hands. I don't think I had ever shaken hands with anyone my own age before. Not that I minded. I was just surprised and had to find a place to put my duffel bag before I could give him my hand. His name was Michael, Michael Egerton. He was taller than I was, and although it was only June, he already had the sort of suntan that would leave his hair white all summer. I knew he couldn't be more than twelve. I wouldn't be twelve until February. If you were twelve you usually had to go to one of the senior cabins across the hill. But his face was old because of the bones under his eyes that showed through the skin.

He introduced me to the man. It was his father but they didn't look alike. His father was a newspaperman and the suitcase they were unpacking had stickers on it that said Rome and Paris, London and Bombay. His father said he would be going back to Europe soon to report about the Army and that Michael would be settled here in camp for a while. I was to keep an eye on Mike, he said, and if he got to France in time, he would try to send us something. He said he could tell that Mike and I were going to be great friends and that I might want to go with Mike to his aunt's when camp was over. I might like to see where Old Mike would be living from now on. It was a beautiful place, he said. I could tell he was getting ready to leave. He had seen Michael make up his bed and fill the locker with clothes, and he was beginning to talk the way everybody does when they are leaving some-where—loud and with a lot of laughing.

He took Michael over to a corner, and I started unpacking my bag. I could see them though and he gave Michael some money, and they talked about how much Michael was going to enjoy the summer and how much bigger he would be when his father got back and how he was to think of his aunt just like a mother. Then Michael reached up and kissed his father. He didn't seem at all embarrassed to do it. They walked back towards me and in a voice louder than before, Mr. Egerton told me again to keep an eye on Old Mike—not that he would need it but it wouldn't hurt.

That was a little funny since Michael was so much bigger than I was, but anyway I said I would because that was what I was supposed to say. And then he left. He said there wouldn't be any need for Mike to walk with him to the car, but Michael wanted to so I watched them walk down the hill together. They stood by the car for a minute, and then Michael kissed him again right in front of all those boys and parents and counselors. Michael stood there until his father's car had passed through the camp gate. He waved once. Then he came on back up the hill.

All eight of the boys in our cabin went to the dining hall together that night, but afterward at campfire Michael and I sat a little way off from the others and talked softly while they sang. He talked some about his father and how he was one of the best war correspondents in the business. It wasn't like bragging because he asked me about my father and what my mother was like. I started to ask him about his mother, but I remembered that he hadn't said anything about her, and I thought she might be dead. But in a while he said very matter-of-factly that his mother didn't live with him and his father, hadn't lived with them for almost a year. That was all. He hadn't seen his mother for a year. He didn't say whether she was sick or what, and I wasn't going to ask.

For a long time after that we didn't say anything. We were sitting on a mound at the foot of a tree just high enough to look down on the other boys around the fire. They were all red in the light, and those furthest from the blaze huddled together and drew their heads down because the nights in the mountains were cold, even in June. They had started singing a song that I didn't know. It was called "Green Grow the Rushes." But Michael knew it and sang and I listened to him. It was almost like church with one person singing against a large soft choir. At the end the camp director stood up and made a speech about this was going to be the best season in the history of Redwood which was the finest camp in the land as it was bound to be with as fine a group of boys and counselors as he had sitting right here in front of him. He said it would be a perfect summer if everybody would practice the Golden Rule twenty-four hours a day and treat everybody like we wanted to be treated— like real men.

When we got back to the cabin, the other boys were already running around in the lantern light naked and slapping each other's behinds with wet towels. But soon the counselor blew the light out, and we got in bed in the dark. Michael was in the bunk over me. We had sentence prayers. Michael asked God to bless his father when he got to France. One boy named

Robin Mickle who was a Catholic said a Hail Mary. It surprised most of the others. Some of them even laughed as if he was telling a joke. Everything quieted down though and we were half asleep when somebody started blowing Taps on a bugle. It woke us all up and we waited in the dark for it to stop so we could sleep.

Michael turned out to be my best friend. Every morning after breakfast everybody was supposed to lie on their beds quietly for Thought Time and think about the Bible, but Michael and I would sit on my bed and talk. I told Michael a lot of things I had never told anyone else. I don't know why I told him. I just wanted him to know everything there was to know about me. It was a long time before I realized that I didn't know much about Michael except what I could see—that he didn't live with his mother and his father was a great war correspondent who was probably back in France now. He just wasn't the kind to tell you a lot. He would listen to everything you had to say as if he wanted to hear it and was glad you wanted to tell him. But then he would change the subject and start talking about baseball or something. He was a very good baseball player, the best on the junior cabin team. Every boy in our cabin was on the team, and it looked as if with Michael pitching we might take the junior title for the Colossians. That was the name of our team. All the athletic teams in camp were named for one of the letters that St. Paul wrote. We practiced every afternoon after rest period, but first we went to the Main Lodge for mail. I got a letter almost every day, and Michael had got two or three from his aunt, but it wasn't until almost three weeks passed that he got the airmail letter from France. There weren't any pictures or souvenirs in it, but I don't suppose Mr. Egerton had too much time for that. He did mention me though I could tell by the way he wrote that he didn't remember my name. Still it was very nice to be thought of by a famous war correspondent. Michael said we could write him a letter together soon and that he would ask his father for a picture.

We wrote him twice but four weeks passed and nothing else came, not from France. I had any number of letters myself and the legal limit of boxes (which was one a week) that I wanted to share with just Michael but had to share with everybody, Robin Mickle included. Worse than the sharing, I dreaded my boxes because I kept thinking they would make me homesick, but with Michael and all the things to do, they never bothered me, and before I expected it, there was only a week of camp left and we would go home. That was why we were playing the semifinals that day—so the winners could be recognized at the Farewell Banquet on the last night of camp. The Colossians were going to play the Ephesians after rest period. We were all in the cabin trying to rest, but everybody was too excited, everybody except Michael who was almost asleep when the camp director walked in and said that Michael Egerton was to go down to the Lodge porch right away as he had visitors. Michael got up and combed his hair, and just before he left he told everybody he would see them at the game and that we were going to win.

The Lodge wasn't too far from our cabin, and I could see him walking down there. A car was parked by the porch. Michael got pretty close to it. Then he stopped. I thought he had forgotten something and was coming back to the cabin, but the car doors opened and a man and a woman got out. I knew it was his mother. He couldn't have looked any more like her. She bent over and kissed him. Then she must have introduced him to the man. She said something and the man stepped up and shook Michael's hand. They started talking. I couldn't hear them and since they weren't doing anything I lay back down and read for a while. Rest period was almost over when I looked again. The car was gone and there was no one in front of the Lodge. It was time for the semifinals, and Michael hadn't showed up. Robin, who was in charge of the Colossians, told me to get Michael wherever he was, and I looked all over camp. He just wasn't there. I didn't have time to go up in the woods behind the cabins, but I yelled and there was no answer. So I had to give up because the game was waiting. Michael never came. A little fat boy named Billy Joe Moffitt took his place and we lost. Everybody wondered what had happened to Michael. I was sure he hadn't left camp with his mother because he would have told somebody first so after the game I ran back ahead of the others. Michael wasn't on his bed. I walked through the hall and opened the bathroom door. He was standing at the window with his back to me. "Mike, why in the world didn't you play?"

He didn't even turn around.

"We lost, Mike."

He just stood there tying little knots in the shade cord. When the others came in from the game, I met them at the door. I told them Michael was sick.

But he went to the campfire with me that night. He didn't say much and I didn't know what to ask him. "Was that your mother this afternoon?"

"Yes."

"What was she doing up here?"

"On a vacation or something."

22

I don't guess I should have asked him but I did. "Who was that with her?"

"Some man. I don't know. Just some man."

It was like every night. We were sitting in our place by the tree. The others were singing and we were listening. Then he started talking very fast.

"My mother said, 'Michael, this is your new father. How do you like having two fathers?' "

Before I could think what to say, he said he was cold and got up and walked back to the cabin. I didn't follow him. I didn't even ask him if he was feeling all right. When I got to the cabin, he was in bed pretending to be asleep, but long after Taps I could hear him turning. I tried to stay awake until he went to sleep. Once I sat up and started to reach out and touch him but I didn't. I was very tired.

All that was a week before the end of camp. The boys in our cabin started talking about him. He had stopped playing ball. He wouldn't swim in the camp meet. He didn't even go on the Sunday hike up to Johnson's Knob. He sat on his bed with his clothes on most of the time. They never did anything nice for him. They were always doing things like tying his shoelaces together. It was no use trying to stop them. All they knew was that Michael Egerton had screwed their chance to be camp baseball champions. They didn't want to know the reason, not even the counselor. And I wasn't going to tell them. They even poured water on his mattress one night and laughed the whole next day about Michael wetting the bed.

The day before we left camp, the counselors voted on a Camp Spirit Cabin. They had kept some sort of record of our activities and athletic events. The cabin with the most Good Camper points usually won. We didn't win. Robin and the others told Michael that he made us lose because he never did anything. They told everybody that Michael Egerton made our cabin lose.

That night we were bathing and getting dressed for the Farewell Banquet. Nobody had expected Michael to go, but without saying anything he started getting dressed. Someone noticed him and said something about Mr. Michael honoring us with his presence at dinner. He had finished dressing when four of the boys took him and tied him between two bunks with his arms stretched out. He didn't fight. He let them treat him like some animal, and he looked as if he was crucified. Then they went to the banquet and left him tied there. I went with them but while they were laughing about hamstringing that damned Michael, I slipped away and went back to untie him. When I got there he had already got loose. I knew he was in the bathroom. I could hear him. I walked to the door and whispered "Mike, it's me." I don't think he heard me. I started to open the door but I didn't. I walked back out and down the hill to the dining hall. They even had the porch lights on, and they had already started singing.

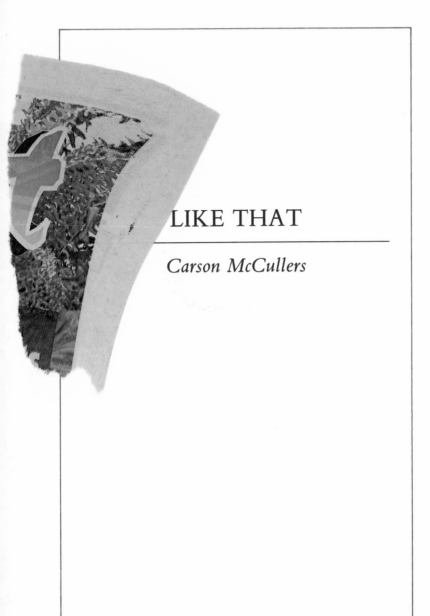

LIKE THAT

Carson McCullers

E ven if Sis is five years older than me and eighteen we used always to be closer and have more fun together than most sisters. It was about the same with us and our brother Dan, too. In the summer we'd all go swimming together. At nights in the wintertime maybe we'd sit around the fire in the living room and play three-handed bridge or Michigan, with everybody putting up a nickel or a dime to the winner. The three of us could have more fun by ourselves than any family I know. That's the way it always was before this.

Not that Sis was playing down to me, either. She's smart as she can be and has read more books than anybody I ever knew—even school teachers. But in High School she never did like to priss up flirty and ride around in cars with girls and pick up the boys and park at the drug store and all that sort of thing. When she wasn't reading she'd just like to play around with me and Dan. She wasn't too grown up to fuss over a chocolate bar in the refrigerator or to stay awake most of Christmas Eve night either, say, with excitement. In some ways it was like I was heaps older than her. Even when Tuck started coming around last summer I'd sometimes have to tell her she shouldn't wear ankle socks because they might go down town or she ought to pluck out her eyebrows above her nose like the other girls do.

In one more year, next June, Tuck'll be graduated from college. He's a lanky boy with an eager look to his face. At college he's so smart he has a free scholarship. He started coming to see Sis the last summer before this one, riding in his family's car when he could get it, wearing crispy white linen suits. He came a lot last year but this summer he came even more often—before he left he was coming around for Sis every night. Tuck's O.K.

It began getting different between Sis and me a while back, I guess, although I didn't notice it at the time. It was only after a certain night this summer that I had the idea that things maybe were bound to end like they are now.

It was late when I woke up that night. When I opened my eyes I thought for a minute it must be about dawn and I was scared when I saw Sis wasn't on her side of the bed. But it was only the moonlight that shone cool looking and white outside the window and made the oak leaves hanging down over the front yard pitch black and separate seeming. It was around the first of September, but I didn't feel hot looking at the moonlight. I pulled the sheet over me and let my eyes roam around the black shapes of the furniture in our room.

I'd waked up lots of times in the night this summer. You see Sis and I have always had this room together and when she would come in and turn on the light to find her nightgown or something it woke me. I liked it. In the summer when school was out I didn't have to get up early in the morning. We would lie and talk sometimes for a good while. I'd like to hear about the places she and Tuck had been or to laugh over different things. Lots of times before that night she had talked to me privately about Tuck just like I was her age—asking me if I thought she should have said this or that when he called and giving me a hug, maybe, after. Sis was really crazy about Tuck. Once she said to me: "He's so lovely—I never in the world thought I'd know anyone like him—"

We would talk about our brother too. Dan's seventeen years old and was planning to take the co-op course at Tech in the fall. Dan had gotten older by this summer. One night he came in at four o'clock and he'd been drinking. Dad sure had it in for him the next week. So he hiked out to the country and camped with some boys for a few days. He used to talk to me and Sis about diesel motors and going away to South America and all that, but by this summer he was quiet and not saying much to anybody in the family. Dan's real tall and thin as a rail. He has bumps on his face now and is clumsy and not very good looking. At nights sometimes I know he wanders all around by himself, maybe going out beyond the city limits sign into the pine woods.

Thinking about such things I lay in bed wondering what time it was and when Sis would be in. That night after Sis and Dan had left I had gone down to the corner with some of the kids in the neighborhood to chunk rocks at the street light and try to kill a bat up there. At first I had the shivers and imagined it was a smallish bat like the kind in Dracula. When I saw it looked just like a moth I didn't care if they killed it or not. I was just sitting there on the curb drawing with a stick on the dusty street when Sis and Tuck rode by slowly in his car. She was sitting over very close to him. They weren't talking or smiling— just riding slowly down the street, sitting close, looking ahead. When they passed and I saw who it was I hollered to them. "Hey, Sis!" I yelled.

The car just went on slowly and nobody hollered back. I just stood there in the middle of the street feeling sort of silly with all the other kids standing around.

Like That

That hateful little old Bubber from down on the other block came up to me. "That your sister?" he asked.

I said yes.

"She sure was sitting up close to her beau," he said.

I was mad all over like I get sometimes. I hauled off and chunked all the rocks in my hand right at him. He's three years younger than me and it wasn't nice, but I couldn't stand him in the first place and he thought he was being so cute about Sis. He started holding his neck and bellering and I walked off and left them and went home and got ready to go to bed.

When I woke up I finally began to think of that too and old Bubber Davis was still in my mind when I heard the sound of a car coming up the block. Our room faces the street with only a short front yard between. You can see and hear everything from the sidewalk and the street. The car was creeping down in front of our walk and the light went slow and white along the walls of the room. It stopped on Sis's writing desk, showed up the books there plainly and half a pack of chewing gum. Then the room was dark and there was only the moonlight outside.

The door of the car didn't open but I could hear them talking. Him, that is. His voice was low and I couldn't catch any words but it was like he was ex-

plaining something over and over again. I never heard
Sis say a word.

I was still awake when I heard the car door open.
I heard her say, "Don't come out." And then the door
slammed and there was the sound of her heels clop-
ping up the walk, fast and light like she was running.

Mama met Sis in the hall outside our room. She
had heard the front door close. She always listens out
for Sis and Dan and never goes to sleep when they're
still out. I sometimes wonder how she can just lie
there in the dark for hours without going to sleep.

"It's one-thirty, Marian," she said. "You ought to
get in before this."

Sis didn't say anything.

"Did you have a nice time?"

That's the way Mama is. I could imagine her standing there with her nightgown blowing out fat around
her and her dead white legs and the blue veins showing, looking all messed up. Mama's nicer when she's
dressed to go out.

"Yes, we had a grand time," Sis said. Her voice
was funny—sort of like the piano in the gym at school,
high and sharp on your ear. Funny.

Mama was asking more questions. Where did they
go? Did they see anybody they knew? All that sort
of stuff. That's the way she is.

"Goodnight," said Sis in that out of tune voice.

She opened the door of our room real quick and closed it. I started to let her know I was awake but changed my mind. Her breathing was quick and loud in the dark and she did not move at all. After a few minutes she felt in the closet for her nightgown and got in the bed. I could hear her crying.

"Did you and Tuck have a fuss?" I asked.

"No," she answered. Then she seemed to change her mind. "Yeah, it was a fuss."

There's one thing that gives me the creeps sure enough—and that's to hear somebody cry. "I wouldn't let it bother me. You'll be making up tomorrow."

The moon was coming in the window and I could see her moving her jaw from one side to the other and staring up at the ceiling. I watched her for a long time. The moonlight was cool looking and there was a wettish wind coming cool from the window. I moved over like I sometimes do to snug up with her, thinking maybe that would stop her from moving her jaw like that and crying.

She was trembling all over. When I got close to her she jumped like I'd pinched her and pushed me over quick and kicked my legs over. "Don't," she said. "Don't."

Maybe Sis had suddenly gone batty, I was thinking. She was crying in a slower and sharper way. I was a little scared and I got up to go to the bathroom a minute. While I was in there I looked out the window, down toward the corner where the street light is. I saw something then that I knew Sis would want to know about.

"You know what?" I asked when I was back in the bed.

She was lying over close to the edge as she could get, stiff. She didn't answer.

"Tuck's car is parked down by the street light. Just drawn up to the curb. I could tell because of the box and the two tires on the back. I could see it from the bathroom window."

She didn't even move.

"He must be just sitting out there. What ails you and him?"

She didn't say anything at all.

"I couldn't see him but he's probably just sitting there in the car under the street light. Just sitting there."

It was like she didn't care or had known it all along. She was as far over the edge of the bed as she could get, her legs stretched out stiff and her hands holding tight to the edge and her face on one arm.

She used always to sleep all sprawled over on my side so I'd have to push at her when it was hot and sometimes turn on the light and draw the line down the middle and show her how she really was on my side. I wouldn't have to draw any line that night, I was thinking. I felt bad. I looked out at the moonlight a long time before I could get to sleep again.

The next day was Sunday and Mama and Dad went in the morning to church because it was the anniversary of the day my aunt died. Sis said she didn't feel well and stayed in bed. Dan was out and I was there by myself so naturally I went into our room where Sis was. Her face was white as the pillow and there were circles under her eyes. There was a muscle jumping on one side of her jaw like she was chewing. She hadn't combed her hair and it flopped over the pillow, glinty red and messy and pretty. She was reading with a book held up close to her face. Her eyes didn't move when I came in. I don't think they even moved across the page.

It was roasting hot that morning. The sun made everything blazing outside so that it hurt your eyes to look. Our room was so hot that you could almost touch the air with your finger. But Sis had the sheet pulled up clear to her shoulders.

"Is Tuck coming today?" I asked. I was trying to say something that would make her look more cheerful.

"Gosh! Can't a person have *any* peace in this house?"

She never did used to say mean things like that out of a clear sky. Mean things, maybe, but not grouchy ones.

"Sure," I said. "Nobody's going to notice you."

I sat down and pretended to read. When footsteps passed on the street Sis would hold on to the book tighter and I knew she was listening hard as she could. I can tell between footsteps easy. I can even tell without looking if the person who passes is colored or not. Colored people mostly make a slurry sound between the steps. When the steps would pass Sis would loosen the hold on the book and bite at her mouth. It was the same way with passing cars.

I felt sorry for Sis. I decided then and there that I never would let any fuss with any boy make me feel or look like that. But I wanted Sis and me to get back like we'd always been. Sunday mornings are bad enough without having any other trouble.

"We fuss a lots less than most sisters do," I said. "And when we do it's all over quick, isn't it?"

She mumbled and kept staring at the same spot on the book.

"That's one good thing," I said.

She was moving her head slightly from side to side—over and over again, with her face not changing. "We never do have any real long fusses like Bubber Davis's two sisters have—"

"No." She answered like she wasn't thinking about what I'd said.

"Not one real one like that since I can remember."

In a minute she looked up the first time. "I remember one," she said suddenly.

"When?"

Her eyes looked green in the blackness under them and like they were nailing themselves into what they saw. "You had to stay in every afternoon for a week. It was a long time ago."

All of a sudden I remembered. I'd forgotten it for a long time. I hadn't wanted to remember. When she said that it came back to me all complete.

It was really a long time ago—when Sis was about thirteen. If I remember right I was mean and even more hardboiled than I am now. My aunt who I'd liked better than all my other aunts put together had had a dead baby and she had died. After the funeral Mama had told Sis and me about it. Always the things I've learned new and didn't like have made me mad— mad clean through and scared.

That wasn't what Sis was talking about, though. It was a few mornings after that when Sis started with what every big girl has each month, and of course I found out and was scared to death. Mama then explained to me about it and what she had to wear. I felt then like I'd felt about my aunt, only ten times worse. I felt different toward Sis, too, and was so mad I wanted to pitch into people and hit.

I never will forget it. Sis was standing in our room

before the dresser mirror. When I remembered her face it was white like Sis's there on the pillow and with the circles under her eyes and the glinty hair to her shoulders—it was only younger.

I was sitting on the bed, biting hard at my knee. "It shows," I said. "It does too!"

She had on a sweater and a blue pleated skirt and she was so skinny all over that it did show a little.

"Anybody can tell. Right off the bat. Just to look at you anybody can tell."

Her face was white in the mirror and did not move.

"It looks terrible. I wouldn't ever ever be like that. It shows and everything."

She started crying then and told Mother and said she wasn't going back to school and such. She cried a long time. That's how ugly and hardboiled I used to be and am still sometimes. That's why I had to stay in the house every afternoon for a week a long time ago. . . .

Tuck came by in his car that Sunday morning before dinner time. Sis got up and dressed in a hurry and didn't even put on any lipstick. She said they were going out to dinner. Nearly every Sunday all of us in the family stay together all day, so that was a little funny. They didn't get home until almost dark. The rest of us were sitting on the front porch drinking ice tea because of the heat when the car drove up again. After they got out of the car Dad, who had been in a very good mood all day, insisted Tuck stay for a glass of tea.

Tuck sat on the swing with Sis and he didn't lean back and his heels didn't rest on the floor—as though he was all ready to get up again. He kept changing the glass from one hand to the other and starting new conversations. He and Sis didn't look at each other except on the sly, and then it wasn't at all like they were crazy about each other. It was a funny look. Almost like they were afraid of something. Tuck left soon.

"Come sit by your Dad a minute, Puss," Dad said. Puss is a nickname he calls Sis when he feels in a specially good mood. He still likes to pet us.

She went and sat on the arm of his chair. She sat stiff like Tuck had, holding herself off a little so Dad's arm hardly went around her waist. Dad smoked his cigar and looked out on the front yard and the trees that were beginning to melt into the early dark.

"How's my big girl getting along these days?" Dad still likes to hug us up when he feels good and treat us, even Sis, like kids.

"O.K.," she said. She twisted a little bit like she wanted to get up and didn't know how to without hurting his feelings.

41

"You and Tuck have had a nice time together this summer, haven't you, Puss?"

"Yeah," she said. She had begun to see-saw her lower jaw again. I wanted to say something but couldn't think of anything.

Dad said: "He ought to be getting back to Tech about now, oughtn't he? When's he leaving?"

"Less than a week," she said. She got up so quick that she knocked Dad's cigar out of his fingers. She didn't even pick it up but flounced on through the front door. I could hear her half running to our room and the sound the door made when she shut it. I knew she was going to cry.

It was hotter than ever. The lawn was beginning to grow dark and the locusts were droning out so shrill and steady that you wouldn't notice them unless you thought to. The sky was bluish grey and the trees in the vacant lot across the street were dark. I kept on sitting on the front porch with Mama and Papa and hearing their low talk without listening to the words. I wanted to go in our room with Sis but I was afraid to. I wanted to ask her what was really the matter. Was hers and Tuck's fuss so bad as that or was it that she was so crazy about him that she was sad because he was leaving? For a minute I didn't think it was either one of those things. I wanted to know but I was scared to ask. I just sat there with the grown

42

people. I never have been so lonesome as I was that night. If ever I think about being sad I just remember how it was then—sitting there looking at the long bluish shadows across the lawn and feeling like I was the only child left in the family and that Sis and Dan were dead or gone for good.

It's October now and the sun shines bright and a little cool and the sky is the color of my turquoise ring. Dan's gone to Tech. So has Tuck gone. It's not at all like it was last fall, though. I come in from High School (I go there now) and Sis maybe is just sitting by the window reading or writing to Tuck or just looking out. Sis is thinner and sometimes to me she looks in the face like a grown person. Or like, in a way, something has suddenly hurt her hard. We don't do any of the things we used to. It's good weather for fudge or for doing so many things. But no she just sits around or goes for long walks in the chilly late afternoon by herself. Sometimes she'll smile in a way that really gripes—like I was such a kid and all. Sometimes I want to cry or to hit her.

But I'm hardboiled as the next person. I can get along by myself if Sis or anybody else wants to. I'm glad I'm thirteen and still wear socks and can do what I please. I don't want to be any older if I'd get like Sis has. But I wouldn't. I wouldn't like any boy in the world as much as she does Tuck. I'd never let any boy or any thing make me act like she does. I'm not going to waste my time and try to make Sis be like she used to be. I get lonesome—sure—but I don't care. I know there's no way I can make myself stay thirteen all my life, but I know I'd never let anything really change me at all—no matter what it is.

I skate and ride my bike and go to the school football games every Friday. But when one afternoon the kids all got quiet in the gym basement and then started telling certain things—about being married and all—I got up quick so I wouldn't hear and went up and played basketball. And when some of the kids said they were going to start wearing lipstick and stockings I said I wouldn't for a hundred dollars.

You see I'd never be like Sis is now. I wouldn't. Anybody could know that if they knew me. I just wouldn't, that's all. I don't want to grow up—if it's like that.

THE WRITER
IN THE FAMILY

E. L. Doctorow

In 1955 my father died with his ancient mother still alive in a nursing home. The old lady was ninety and hadn't even known he was ill. Thinking the shock might kill her, my aunts told her that he had moved to Arizona for his bronchitis. To the immigrant generation of my grandmother, Arizona was the American equivalent of the Alps, it was where you went for your health. More accurately, it was where you went if you had the money. Since my father had failed in all the business enterprises of his life this was the aspect of the news my grandmother dwelled on, that he had finally had some success. And so it came about that as we mourned him at home in our stocking feet, my grandmother was bragging to her cronies about her son's new life in the dry air of the desert.

My aunts had decided on their course of action without consulting us. It meant neither my mother nor my brother nor I could visit Grandma, because we were supposed to have moved west too, a family, after all. My brother Harold and I didn't mind—it was always a nightmare at the old people's home, where they all sat around staring at us while we tried to make conversation with Grandma. She looked terrible, had numbers of ailments, and her mind wandered. Not seeing her was not a disappointment for my mother either; she had never gotten along with the old woman and did not visit when she could have. But what was disturbing was that my aunts had acted in the manner of that side of the family, making government on everyone's behalf, the true citizens by blood and the lesser citizens by marriage. It was exactly this attitude that had tormented my mother all her married life. She claimed Jack's family had never accepted her. She had battled them for twenty-five years as an outsider.

A few weeks after the end of our ritual mourning my Aunt Frances phoned us from her home in Larchmont. Aunt Frances was the wealthier of my father's sisters. Her husband was a lawyer, and both her sons were at Amherst. She had called to say that Grandma was asking why she didn't hear from Jack. I had answered the phone. "You're the writer in the family," my aunt said. "Your father had so much faith in you. Would you mind making up something? Send it to

me and I'll read it to her. She won't know the difference."

That evening, at the kitchen table, I pushed my
homework aside and composed a letter. I tried to
imagine my father's response to his new life. He had
never been west. He had never traveled anywhere. In
his generation the great journey was from the working
class to the professional class, and he hadn't managed
that, either. But he loved New York, where he had
been born and lived his life, and he was always dis-
covering new things about it. He especially loved the
old parts of the city below Canal Street, where he
would find ships' chandlers or firms that wholesaled
in spices and teas. He was a salesman for an appliance
jobber with accounts all over the city. He liked to
bring home rare cheeses or exotic foreign vegetables
that were sold only in certain neighborhoods. Once he
brought home a barometer, another time an antique
ship's telescope in a wooden case with a brass snap.

"Dear Mama," I wrote, "Arizona is beautiful. The
sun shines all day and the air is warm and I feel better
than I have in years. The desert is not as barren as
you would expect, but filled with wild flowers and
cactus plants and peculiar crooked trees that look like
men holding their arms out. You can see great dis-
tances in whatever direction you turn and to the west

is a range of mountains maybe fifty miles from here, but in the morning with the sun on them you can see the snow on their crests."

My aunt called some days later and told me it was when she read this letter aloud to the old lady that the full effect of Jack's death came over her. She had to excuse herself and went out in the parking lot to cry. "I wept so," she said. "I felt such terrible longing for him. You're so right, he loved to go places, he loved life, he loved everything."

We began trying to organize our lives. My father had borrowed money against his insurance and there was very little left. Some commissions were still due but it didn't look as if his firm would honor them. There was a couple of thousand dollars in a savings bank that had to be maintained there until the estate was settled. The lawyer involved was Aunt Frances's husband and he was very proper. "The estate!" my mother muttered, gesturing as if to pull out her hair. "The estate!" She applied for a job part-time in the admissions office of the hospital where my father's terminal illness had been diagnosed, and where he had spent some months until they had sent him home to die. She knew a lot of the doctors and staff and she had learned "from bitter experience," as she told them, about the hospital routine. She was hired.

The Writer in the Family

I hated that hospital, it was dark and grim and full of tortured people. I thought it was masochistic of my mother to seek out a job there but did not tell her so.

We lived in an apartment on the corner of 175th Street and the Grand Concourse, one flight up. Three rooms. I shared the bedroom with my brother. It was jammed with furniture because when my father had required a hospital bed in the last weeks of his illness we had moved some of the living room pieces into the bedroom and made over the living room for him. We had to navigate bookcases, beds, a gateleg table, bureaus, a record player and radio console, stacks of 78 albums, my brother's trombone and music stand, and so on. My mother continued to sleep on the convertible sofa in the living room that had been their bed before his illness. The two rooms were connected by a narrow hall made even narrower by bookcases along the wall. Off the hall was a small kitchen and dinette and a bathroom. There were lots of appliances in the kitchen—broiler, toaster, pressure cooker, counter-top dishwasher, blender—that my father had gotten through his job at cost. A treasured phrase in our house: *at cost*. But most of these fixtures went unused because my mother did not care for them. Chromium devices with timers or gauges that required the reading of elaborate instructions were not for her. They were in part responsible for the awful clutter of our lives and now she wanted to get rid of them. "We're being buried," she said. "Who needs them!"

So we agreed to throw out or sell anything inessential. While I found boxes for the appliances and my brother tied the boxes with twine, my mother opened my father's closet and took out his clothes. He had several suits because as a salesman he needed to look his best. My mother wanted us to try on his suits to see which of them could be altered and used. My brother refused to try them on. I tried on one jacket, which was too large for me. The lining inside the sleeves chilled my arms and the vaguest scent of my father's being came to me.

"This is way too big," I said.

"Don't worry," my mother said. "I had it cleaned. Would I let you wear it if I hadn't?"

It was the evening, the end of winter, and the snow was coming down on the windowsill and melting as it settled. The ceiling bulb glared on a pile of my father's suits and trousers on hangers flung across the bed in the shape of a dead man. We refused to try on anything more and my mother began to cry.

"What are you crying for?" my brother shouted. "You wanted to get rid of things, didn't you?"

A few weeks later my aunt phoned again and said she thought it would be necessary to have another letter from Jack. Grandma had fallen out of her chair and bruised herself and was very depressed.

"How long does this go on?" my mother said.

"It's not so terrible," my aunt said, "for the little time left to make things easier for her."

My mother slammed down the phone. "He can't even die when he wants to!" she cried. "Even death comes second to Mama! What are they afraid of, the shock will kill her? Nothing can kill her. She's indestructible! A stake through the heart couldn't kill her!"

When I sat down in the kitchen to write the letter I found it more difficult than the first one. "Don't watch me," I said to my brother. "It's hard enough."

"You don't have to do something just because someone wants you to," Harold said. He was two years older than me and had started at City College; but when my father became ill he had switched to night school and gotten a job in a record store.

"Dear Mama," I wrote, "I hope you're feeling well. We're all fit as a fiddle. The life here is good and the people are very friendly and informal. Nobody wears suits and ties here. Just a pair of slacks and a short-sleeved shirt. Perhaps a sweater in the evening. I have bought into a very successful radio and record business and I'm doing very well. You remember Jack's Electric, my old place on Forty-third Street? Well, now it's Jack's Arizona Electric and we have a line of television sets as well."

I sent that letter off to my Aunt Frances, and as we all knew she would, she phoned soon after. My brother held his hand over the mouthpiece. "It's Frances with her latest review," he said.

"Jonathan? You're a very talented young man. I just wanted to tell you what a blessing your letter was. Her whole face lit up when I read the part about Jack's store. That would be an excellent way to continue."

"Well I hope I don't have to do this anymore, Aunt Frances. It's not very honest."

Her tone changed. "Is your mother there? Let me talk to her."

"She's not here," I said.

"Tell her not to worry," my aunt said. "A poor old lady who has never wished anything but the best for her will soon die."

I did not repeat this to my mother, for whom it would have been one more in the family anthology of unforgivable remarks. But then I had to suffer it myself for the possible truth it might embody. Each side defended its position with rhetoric, but I, who wanted peace, rationalized the snubs and rebuffs each inflicted on the other, taking no stands, like my father himself.

Years ago his life had fallen into a pattern of business failures and missed opportunities. The great debate between his family on the one side, and my mother Ruth on the other, had to do with whose fault was this: who was responsible for the fact that he had not lived up to anyone's expectations?

As to the prophecies, when spring came my mother's prevailed: Grandma was still alive.

One balmy Sunday my mother and brother and I took the bus to the Beth El cemetery in New Jersey to visit my father's grave. It was situated on a slight rise. We stood looking over rolling fields embedded with monuments. Here and there processions of black cars wound their way through the lanes, or clusters of people stood at open graves. My father's grave was planted with tiny shoots of evergreen but it lacked a headstone. We had chosen one and paid for it and then the stonecutters had gone on strike. Without a headstone my father did not seem to be honorably dead. He didn't seem to me properly buried.

My mother gazed at the plot beside his, reserved for her coffin. "They were always too fine for other people," she said. "Even in the old days on Stanton Street. They put on airs. Nobody was ever good enough for them. Finally Jack himself was not good enough for them. Except to get them things wholesale. Then he was good enough for them."

"Mom, please," my brother said.

"If I had known. Before I ever met him he was tied to his mama's apron strings. And Essie's apron strings were like chains, let me tell you. We had to live where we could be near them for the Sunday visits. Every Sunday, that was my life, a visit to Mamaleh. Whatever she knew I wanted, a better apartment, a stick of furniture, a summer camp for the boys, she spoke against it. You know your father, every decision had to be considered and reconsidered. And nothing changed. Nothing ever changed."

She began to cry. We sat her down on a nearby bench. My brother walked off to read the names on stones. I looked at my mother, who was crying and I went off after my brother.

"Mom's still crying," I said. "Shouldn't we do something?"

"It's all right," he said. "It's what she came here for."

"Yes," I said, and then a sob escaped from my throat. "But I feel like crying too."

My brother Harold put his arm around me. "Look at this old black stone here," he said. "The way it's carved. You can see the changing fashion in monuments—just like everything else. "

Somewhere in this time I began dreaming of my father. Not the robust father of my childhood, the handsome man with healthy pink skin and brown eyes and a mustache and the thinning hair parted in the middle. My dead father. We were taking him home from the hospital. It was understood that he had come back from death. This was amazing and joyous. On the other hand, he was terribly mysteriously damaged, or, more accurately, spoiled and unclean. He was very yellowed and debilitated by his death, and there were no guarantees that he wouldn't soon die again. He seemed aware of this and his entire personality was changed. He was angry and impatient with all of us. We were trying to help him in some way, struggling to get him home, but something prevented us, something we had to fix, a tattered suitcase that had sprung open, some mechanical thing: he had a car but it wouldn't start; or the car was made of wood; or his clothes, which had become too large for him, had caught in the door. In one version he was all bandaged and as we tried to lift him from his wheelchair into a taxi the bandage began to unroll and catch in the spokes of the wheelchair. This seemed to be some unreasonableness on his part. My mother looked on sadly and tried to get him to cooperate.

That was the dream. I shared it with no one. Once when I woke, crying out, my brother turned on the light. He wanted to know what I'd been dreaming but I pretended I didn't remember. The dream made me feel guilty. I felt guilty *in* the dream too because my enraged father knew we didn't want to live with him. The dream represented us taking him home, or trying to, but it was nevertheless understood by all of us that he was to live alone. He was this derelict back from death, but what we were doing was taking him to some place where he would live by himself without help from anyone until he died again.

At one point I became so fearful of this dream that I tried not to go to sleep. I tried to think of good things about my father and to remember him before his illness. He used to call me matey. "Hello, matey," he would say when he came home from work. He always wanted us to go someplace—to the store, to the park, to a ball game. He loved to walk. When I went walking with him he would say: "Hold your shoulders back, don't slump. Hold your head up and look at the world. Walk as if you meant it!" As he strode down the street his shoulders moved from side to side, as if he was hearing some kind of cakewalk.

He moved with a bounce. He was always eager to see what was around the corner.

The next request for a letter coincided with a special occasion in our house: My brother Harold had met a girl he liked and had gone out with her several times. Now she was coming to our house for dinner.

We had prepared for this for days, cleaning everything in sight, giving the house a going-over, washing the dust of disuse from the glasses and good dishes. My mother came home early from work to get the dinner going. We opened the gateleg table in the living room and brought in the kitchen chairs. My mother spread the table with a laundered white cloth and put out her silver. It was the first family occasion since my father's illness.

I liked my brother's girlfriend a lot. She was a thin girl with very straight hair and she had a terrific smile. Her presence seemed to excite the air. It was astounding to see a living breathing girl in our house. She looked around and what she said was, "Oh, I've never seen so many books!" While she and my brother sat at the table my mother was in the kitchen putting the food into serving bowls and I was going from the kitchen to the living room, kidding around like a waiter, with a white cloth over my arm and a high style of service, placing the serving dish of green beans on the table with a flourish. In the kitchen my mother's eyes were sparkling. She looked at me and nodded and mimed the words: "She's adorable!"

My brother suffered himself to be waited on. He was wary of what we might say. He kept glancing at the girl—her name was Susan—to see if we met with her approval. She worked in an insurance office and was taking courses in accounting at City College. Harold was under a terrible strain but he was excited and happy too. He had bought a bottle of Concord grape wine to go with the roast chicken. He held up his glass and proposed a toast. My mother said, "To good health and happiness," and we all drank, even I. At that moment the phone rang and I went into the bedroom to get it.

"Jonathan? This is your Aunt Frances. How is everyone?"

"Fine, thank you."

"I want to ask one last favor of you. I need a letter from Jack. Your Grandma's very ill. Do you think you can?"

"Who is it?" my mother called from the living room.

"O.K., Aunt Frances," I said quickly. "I have to go now, we're eating dinner." And I hung up the phone.

"It was my friend Louie," I said, sitting back down.

60

"He didn't know the math pages to review."

The dinner was very fine. Harold and Susan washed the dishes and by the time they were done my mother and I had folded up the gateleg table and put it back against the wall and I had swept the crumbs up with the carpet sweeper. We all sat and talked and listened to records for a while and then my brother took Susan home. The evening had gone very well.

Once when my mother wasn't home my brother had pointed out something: the letters from Jack were not really necessary. "What is this ritual?" he said, holding his palms up. "Grandma is almost totally blind, she's half deaf and crippled. Does the situation really call for a literary composition? Does it need verisimilitude? Would the old lady know the difference if she was read the phone book?"

"Then why did Aunt Frances ask me?"

"That is the question, Jonathan. Why did she? After all, she could write the letter herself—what difference would it make? And if not Frances why not Frances's sons, the Amherst students? They should have learned by now to write."

"But they're not Jack's sons," I said.

"That's exactly the point," my brother said. "The idea is *service*. Dad used to bust his balls getting them things wholesale, getting them deals on things. Frances of Westchester really needed things at cost. And Aunt Molly. And Aunt Molly's husband, and Aunt Molly's ex-husband. Grandma, if she needed an errand done. He was always on the hook for something. They never thought his time was important. They never thought every favor he got was one he had to pay back. Appliances, records, watches, china, opera tickets, any goddamn thing. Call Jack."

"It was a matter of pride to him to be able to do things for them," I said. "To have connections."

"Yeah, I wonder why," my brother said. He looked out the window.

Then suddenly it dawned upon me that I was being implicated.

"You should use your head more," my brother said.

Yet I agreed once again to write a letter from the desert and so I did. I mailed it off to Aunt Frances. A few days later, when I came home from school, I thought I saw her sitting in her car in front of our house. She drove a black Buick Roadmaster, a very large clean car with whitewall tires. It was Aunt Frances, all right. She blew the horn when she saw me. I went over and leaned in at the window.

"Hello, Jonathan," she said. "I haven't long. Can you get in the car?"

"Mom's not home," I said. "She's working."

"I know that. I came to talk to you."

"Would you like to come upstairs?"

"I can't, I have to get back to Larchmont. Can you get in for a moment, please?"

I got in the car. My Aunt Frances was a very pretty white-haired woman, very elegant, and she wore tasteful clothes. I had always liked her and from the time I was a child she had enjoyed pointing out to everyone that I looked more like her son than Jack's. She wore white gloves and held the steering wheel and looked straight ahead as she talked, as if the car were in traffic and not sitting at the curb.

"Jonathan," she said, "there is your letter on the seat. Needless to say I didn't read it to Grandma. I'm giving it back to you and I won't ever say a word to anyone. This is just between us. I never expected cruelty from you. I never thought you were capable of doing something so deliberately cruel and perverse."

I said nothing.

"Your mother has very bitter feelings and now I see she has poisoned you with them. She always resented the family. She is a very strong-willed, selfish person."

"No she isn't," I said.

"I wouldn't expect you to agree. She drove poor

Jack crazy with her demands. She always had the highest aspirations and he could never fulfill them to her satisfaction. When he still had his store, he kept your mother's brother, who drank, on salary. After the war when he began to make a little money he had to buy Ruth a mink jacket because she was so desperate to have one. He had debts to pay but she wanted a mink. He was a very special person, my brother, he should have accomplished something special, but he loved your mother and devoted his life to her. And all she ever thought about was keeping up with the Joneses."

I watched the traffic going up the Grand Concourse. A bunch of kids were waiting at the bus stop at the corner. They had put their books on the ground and were horsing around.

"I'm sorry I have to descend to this," Aunt Frances said. "I don't like talking about people this way. If I have nothing good to say about someone, I'd rather not say anything. How is Harold?"

"Fine."

"Did he help you write this marvelous letter?"

"No."

After a moment she said more softly, "How are you all getting along?"

"Fine."

"I would invite you up for Passover if I thought your mother would accept."

I didn't answer.

She turned on the engine. "I'll say good-bye now, Jonathan. Take your letter. I hope you give some time to thinking about what you've done."

That evening when my mother came home from work I saw that she wasn't as pretty as my Aunt Frances. I usually thought my mother was a good-looking woman, but I saw now that she was too heavy and that her hair was undistinguished.

"Why are you looking at me?" she said.

"I'm not."

"I learned something interesting today," my mother said. "We may be eligible for a V.A. pension because of the time your father spent in the Navy."

That took me by surprise. Nobody had ever told me my father was in the Navy.

"In World War I," she said, "he went to Webb's Naval Academy on the Harlem River. He was training to be an ensign. But the war ended and he never got his commission."

After dinner the three of us went through the closets looking for my father's papers, hoping to find some proof that he could be filed with the Veterans Administration. We came up with two things, a Victory Medal, which my brother said everyone got for being in the service during the Great War, and an astounding sepia photograph of my father and his shipmates on the deck of a ship. They were dressed in bell-bottoms and T-shirts and armed with mops and pails, brooms and brushes.

"I never knew this," I found myself saying. "I never knew this."

"You just don't remember," my brother said.

I was able to pick out my father. He stood at the end of the row, a thin, handsome boy with a full head of hair, a mustache, and an intelligent smiling countenance.

"He had a joke," my mother said. "They called their training ship the S.S. *Constipation* because it never moved."

Neither the picture nor the medal was proof of anything, but my brother thought a duplicate of my father's service record had to be in Washington somewhere and that it was just a matter of learning how to go about finding it.

"The pension wouldn't amount to much," my mother said. "Twenty or thirty dollars. But it would certainly help."

I took the picture of my father and his shipmates and propped it against the lamp at my bedside. I looked into his youthful face and tried to relate it to the Father I knew. I looked at the picture a long time. Only gradually did my eye connect it to the set of Great Sea Novels in the bottom shelf of the bookcase a few feet away. My father had given that set to me: it was uniformly bound in green with gilt lettering and it included works by Melville, Conrad, Victor Hugo, and Captain Marryat. And lying across the top of the books, jammed in under the sagging shelf above, was his old ship's telescope in its wooden case with the brass snap.

I thought how stupid, and imperceptive, and self-centered I had been never to have understood while he was alive what my father's dream for his life had been.

On the other hand, I had written in my last letter from Arizona—the one that had so angered Aunt Frances—something that might someday allow me, the writer in the family, to soften my judgment of myself. I will conclude by giving the letter here in its entirety.

Dear Mama,

This will be my final letter to you since I have been told by the doctors that I am dying.

I have sold my store at a very fine profit and am sending Frances a check for five thousand dollars to be deposited in your account. My present to you, Mamaleh. Let Frances show you the passbook.

As for the nature of my ailment, the doctors haven't told me what it is, but I know that I am simply dying of the wrong life. I should never have come to the desert. It wasn't the place for me.

I have asked Ruth and the boys to have my body cremated and the ashes scattered in the ocean.

Your loving son,
Jack

A DISTANT BELL

Elizabeth Enright

The year after my father and mother were divorced, my father, who got me in the summers, took me to a town on the Cape called Harbor Landing. It was a fish-smelling, gull-squeaking, heterogeneous sort of town heaped up on the hills and bluffs that commanded a view of the harbor with its fringe of docks and shanties. Artists swarmed there in the summertime.

The name of our hotel was "The Nippanoggin Inn." The name was the jauntiest thing about it; indeed it was the only jaunty thing. The clapboarded building was painted egg-yolk yellow and had a mansard roof. The tiers of porches on the harbor side were stocked with wooden rocking chairs that rocked untenanted when the east wind blew, and that summer they rocked often.

"All right, Susie, this is yours, right next to mine," my father said, as if his hearty tone could liven up the room he led me into. Through the two windows facing me I saw the gray, littered harbor. The scrim curtains were limp and blotched with liver spots of rust, and looped on a hook beside the right-hand window there was a coil of knotted rope.

"What's that thing for?" I said, unbuttoning my coat.

"Well, *not* to hang yourself with, Sue! Quite the opposite. That's your own personal fire escape. But I'm certain you won't need to use it unless you're planning to elope."

My father, I sensed, was trying hard. I smiled obligingly, though I thought he could not know much about me if he didn't know I loathed most boys and planned never to marry; and it was no joking matter. I was eleven years old, with straight red hair, and skinny knees that jutted out above my socks. I felt uncomfortable with my father, and I think he did with me. We did not know each other very well, having lost track of each other, rather, in the years just past.

"Well, I hope you're going to be comfortable here, Susie. It's not what I'd call . . . it's not a luxurious bower exactly. But then we'll be outdoors a lot," he said, brightening. "Now why don't you unpack, get settled? I will, too, and then we'll go out and explore the town, shall we?"

"All right," I said.

When he had gone I went to the iron bedstead and

sat down. The mattress felt as if it had been stuffed with the unclaimed laundry of former guests. I examined my new furniture: bureau, washstand, small lame table by the window. There were two chairs; my father had put my suitcase on one of them, and instead of a closet there was a cretonne curtain that hung from a rod at one side of the room. I supposed that by the time I returned to the city all these things would have become familiar and accepted, a sort of home, but it was hard to believe just then.

I got up and opened my suitcase and took out the reading material that lay on my folded clothes: a copy of *John Martin's Book,* a copy of the *Atlantic Monthly.* One by one I lifted out my dresses and hung them on the jangling hangers behind the curtain. When I was putting my underclothes into a bureau drawer I caught sight of my face in the mirror.

"Hideous mule," I said to it, and then leaned forward with interest to watch as a tear rolled slowly down one cheek.

There was a knock at the door. I hastily disposed of the tear with a pair of socks, and turned to face my father.

He looked greatly refreshed, and there was a whiff of something new about him: a whiff of something to drink, I thought. I was glad. If he felt better, then I felt better, too.

73

The town was remarkably ugly, I remember that. Ugly in spite of the elms, in spite of the fine old houses, in spite of the harbor. It was ugly with people. At that time of day the trippers from Boston, with their celluloid visors and boat-burned faces and paper bags and cameras and children, poured into the main street. All their faces were in motion as they talked, laughed, ogled, jeered, and, dipping things out of the brown paper bags, chewed, gobbled, sucked, and spat out pits. All their eyes roved and darted eagerly, looking for artists, for the outlandish (and perhaps scandalous?) artists they had come to see; and the artists obliged. Not only had they left their traces everywhere, palette-knife scrapings on elm bark and curbstone and fence picket, but they were themselves boldly in evidence. Sporting sandals and beards, Navajo necklaces and earrings like buckets, they walked along the street in loud groups or sat at their easels in full view, together or alone, painting the same outpainted wharves, boats, and old characters that had been their subjects for years; but painting them, now, with a difference.

"Don't look like no boat to me, looks more like my gram-mother's flatiron," remarked an onlooker, ramming peanuts into his mouth, as his boiled-red wife shook with laughter and shifted the baby to her other hip.

More and more people clogged the street.

"Let's get out of this. They may stampede," my father said. He took my hand and tucked it in his arm and we plowed a course through the crowd, turned down a side street, and came to the harbor. It was low tide, and the exposed marly sand was studded with shells and bits of interesting trash. I picked up an old tin fork and a piece of green bottle glass.

"We'll find the bathing beach tomorrow," my father promised.

That night after dinner he produced a parcheesi board and we had a long satisfying game which I won. Afterward when I lay down on my remarkable mattress I fell asleep almost at once and slept for eleven hours, and when I woke up the windows were full of sun.

My father and I were alike in this way; we didn't care for talk at breakfast time. My mother was the opposite; she would begin to burble like a house wren the moment she opened her eyes. But now, alone with my father, I sat in silence reading while I ate, a habit I was never allowed to indulge at home. My father allowed it because he wanted to read himself; the arrangement suited us both.

During the morning he worked in his room, and I would sit at my little lame table painting pictures of sorceresses and queens. When I looked out the window I saw the harbor, the fussy boats, the swinging gulls. Next door I could hear the clacking of the typewriter, sometimes hurried and voluble; sometimes hesitant. There would be a long exasperated pause, a tentative tap and tap-tap, another pause, then sometimes the sound of an exclamation and the dry crumpling of paper.

At noon he would knock on my door and we went off to swim at the bathing beach where the water was clean and dazzling. He was an excellent swimmer, my father, and liked to swim well out and away from the shore. I used to watch with real anxiety as his head and rhythmically flailing arms grew more and more distant, were nearly lost to view. I could not settle down to my enjoyment until he had returned from that first long sortie into the blue.

"Don't worry about me, Sue," he said. "I always turn back as soon as I see Spain."

He told me of the creatures he had met along the way: the plaice fish who gave him tips on the horses, "Sea horses, that is," he said; and the jellyfish named Mrs. Cadwallader, "a Main Line jellyfish. But she can't find a corset to fit her."

He made short shrift of my formless side stroke and spent hours teaching me the crawl and the trudgen: accomplishments I cherish to this day.

It was always rather late when we returned to the

inn. Sometimes they had run out of corn on the cob. The other occupants of the dining room, mostly in aging pairs, bowed chewing above their plates. The stained-glass clerestory above sent down a churchly light, and imposed a churchly hush. We spoke in low tones.

"Southern fried chicken," grumbled my father, sawing away at a drumstick. "Southern fried buzzard, more likely. Southern fried emu."

Besides the chicken there was always roast beef *au jus* on the menu, and Boston scrod. The beef was served in green-gray slices chilled at the edges, and I could never bring myself to try anything called scrod. The vegetables came in little extra dishes: succotash awash in milk, potatoes mashed with water and flung onto the dish with a ladle.

"Thank God for catsup," my father used to say; but I did not care for catsup. I was perfectly happy, though, on my diet of bread and butter and milk and ice cream.

"I don't suppose I ought to allow it," my father said helplessly. "Don't they . . . doesn't your mother make you eat everything at home?"

"Oh, they can't *make* me, Daddy," I assured him. "I have the appetite of a bird."

When he didn't go back to work we spent the afternoons together; going on expeditions in the little roadster he had hired, walking along the ocean shore where surf gnawed the beaches, or searching in the pine woods for Indian pipes. When he played golf I walked the course with him and was his caddy.

And I had found a friend for the days when he was busy: a girl named Avalon Bray, who lived near the beach. She was two years older than I was, and in certain ways seemed older than that; I noticed that she looked at any boys we saw with a worried, wistful glance. As yet the boys did not respond. Avalon wore braces on her teeth that looked like lead, her hair was a mess, and she had not "filled out"; instead she looked *pulled* out, as if she had just recently been stretched from something smaller.

Still, she was a companion, and we spent hours playing in the sea together, wandering on the tide flats that smelled of chowder and crackled with the occupations of crabs.

"Gee, Sue, I think your father's *cute!*" she startled me by saying, one day.

"Cute? Men can't be cute," I said.

"Sure they can. Some. *He* is. He's *good*-looking."

I knew that. It was strange. I could not tell whether my mother was pretty or not; her face was simply Mother's Face. But I knew my father was handsome, and could see it.

At night, after dinner, he and I played our games,

78

parcheesi or dominoes, and sometimes, if I begged him, he would tell me a story as he had often done when I was younger. He was very good at this and could spin a story out to last for hours. I went to bed late those nights, and often the last thing I heard before I slept was the irregular castanet-note of his typewriter.

All those days were fair. I remember them as being fair. The weather changed when Mrs. Fenwick came: the morning of the day she came.

When I woke up that day the east wind was blowing; the window curtains tossed listlessly, and the noise of gulls was sharp in the room. At breakfast my father was even more silent than usual. Perhaps the weather and the constant companionship of an eleven-year-old daughter were beginning to chafe his spirits.

His work went badly that morning; I could tell by the silences. The rain began to spit at ten; and I upset a jar of crimson madder on the rug.

At lunch he was morose. The vegetable was spinach. "Or is it kelp?" he wondered; and he said his coffee tasted as if there were limpets in it.

Afterward he returned to work, and I went to Avalon's house, which was wracked with the noise of younger brothers. We locked ourselves in her room with a supply of graham crackers and peanut butter, and she told me the facts of life.

"My heavens, Sue, you mean you honestly didn't *know?*"

"Not quite. Not exactly," I admitted, fascinated and appalled. Could I believe her, or was she crazy?

"Oh, my heavens, you're such a *baby!*" she cried, suddenly exasperated by my youth. With this beginning we managed a quarrel, and soon I left the house, upset on several counts.

At the inn I found my father in the lobby reading the paper.

"Couldn't stand that damned room another second," he said. "And I think the typewriter has rabies. It bit me. Where's what's-her-name? Avalon?"

"Oh, we're mad."

"What about?"

"Oh, nothing much," I said, glad of a sudden stir at the outer entrance of the lobby.

Calvin, the elderly bellboy, hobbled in with a load of Vuitton luggage. Behind him came two women, two new guests. One of them was old, stooped and tremulous, but the other, on whose arm she was leaning, was tall and commanding. She gave an immediate effect of confidence, perhaps accentuated by the contrast between herself and her companion. She also gave an effect of luxury, of well-being; all her appurtenances seemed exactly right for her: the fur scarf, the large hat with a veil, the big pearls on her ear lobes, and most of all the soft expensive aura of perfume that breathed from her.

"You sit down here, Auntie," she said to the older woman. "I'll sign the register." Her voice was rich and confident, too. I thought of the word *contralto,* although I was not certain of its meaning.

"Daddy," I said. "It's stopped raining. Can we go over to the surf now? Daddy? Can we?"

Though he stood facing me, my father was looking intently from the corners of his eyes at the tall woman signing the register. He did not answer.

"Daddy!" I repeated sharply.

At this the tall woman turned suddenly and looked over her shoulder at me, at him. She smiled a warm, friendly smile at me, at him. The fur stole slipped from her shoulders to the floor, and my father sprang forward.

"Oh, thank you so much! How clumsy of me!"

My father bowed and smiled, then turned to me lightheartedly. "All right, Mrs. Murphy, what do you say we go for a spin?" This was a name he called me when he was feeling cheerful.

In the dining room that evening, we saw that the newcomers had a table near the door. The tall one greeted us as we went by, and I noticed that my father glanced in her direction more than once during the meal.

Afterward, though the air was gray and damp, we went through the lounge to the veranda, as we did every evening. My father liked to smoke there after dinner.

He took a cigar from his pocket and clipped the end; absently he slipped the cigar band off and handed it to me. "Here's the ring you ordered, Mrs. Murphy."

I took it but did not put it on my finger. Cigar-band rings were for people of seven or less; I had finished with them years ago.

There was a sound of women's voices in the lounge, and I knew who was coming because of the smell of perfume that came first.

The tall woman held the screen door open for her aunt.

"I hope we're not disturbing you?"

"Of course not!" said my father quickly, standing up. He moved two rockers to the rail near ours, then introduced himself and me.

"And I am Meta Fenwick," she said. "Mrs. Abel Fenwick. And this is my aunt, Miss Currier."

We all sat down, Miss Currier taking a while to settle, cocooning herself against the damp; requiring a cushion from the lounge. Her niece opened a beaded bag and took out a cigarette case. Gold. And in it were flat little cigarettes with golden tips.

"I didn't think they'd care to have me smoking in the lounge!" she confided, smiling at my father. "But I simply must have my cigarette after dinner. I am an addict!"

My father held a light for her; and soon there was another smoke to mingle with his: light, musky, rather sweet. I left my rocker and sat on the rail so I could watch her better.

"Honey, don't you *fall*," said Mrs. Fenwick, but not as if she were really worried; just to be polite.

She was an ample woman, not fat or plump, but *ample*. She was tall, as I have said, with a large bosom, and a creamy skin. Her gray eyes were long and luminous, her glossy hair was marcelled under a hair net, and there was a deep dimple in her chin. She laughed as often as she did, I suspect, because her teeth were flawless; and how well I remember that laugh! It had an easy, gratified quality. Everything about her was smooth, luxurious, unhurried.

Examining my memory of her I can see, now, that she was dead ripe: a woman at the last perfect moment before the gray begins in the hair and the soft flesh becomes a little too soft. . . . It surprises me that I hated her so soon. She did her best to win me; she was kind, and I was not often given to hatred.

After that evening nothing was the same again. On the few days when we could swim, Mrs. Fenwick swam with us. She was a good golfer, too, so most of my father's afternoons were spent with her on the course; and now when we played our evening games there were three of us; sometimes four, though Miss Currier had become, as such old ladies often do, a background type.

("Poor Auntie, she's had so little. I'm all the family she has left. And she is all that I have . . . now."

"Your husband?" murmured my father.

"I've been a widow for three years," she told him gently.)

So I spent more and more time with Avalon. We had patched our quarrel up as we patched up many others. Our quarrels were not important; but neither was our friendship. We were nothing to each other but a means of killing time. Avalon, especially, was restive; she longed to be off and away in the next exciting part of her life. All of her was ready for it but her looks, poor thing. My childishness must have been a constant reminder and goad to her.

One day we took a picnic (with Mrs. Fenwick) to a place called Kettle Cove. Avalon went with us. All of us swam, but she and I kept on till we were sodden, as we always did. It was noon when we came out. Mrs. Fenwick and my father lay propped on their elbows on the sand, talking in low voices.

"Look at them," whispered Avalon, giving me a

jab. "Your father's got a case on her, they've got a case on each *other*. Anyone can tell." She giggled, and suddenly, against my will, I thought of the things she had told me in her room that day.

"Oh, they have not. You're dis*gus*ting! Go to hell!" I whispered furiously. But we had to sacrifice that quarrel; after all, we were stuck there for the day, and with them.

As we got out of the car at the inn I heard Mrs. Fenwick murmur to my father: "We don't care what the tabbies in the rocking chairs are saying, do we?"

That evening she came out on the veranda to smoke her cigarette, wrapped in a pale-blue cashmere coat.

"Autumn is in the air," my father said.

"Yes, too soon . . . It always comes too soon." She looked at me perched on the railing, trying not to shiver. "Why, Susie dear, your teeth are chattering. Come here, come under my wing."

She held out the edges of her coat and a warm gust of perfume came from her. Half fascinated, half repelled, I allowed myself to be drawn into this shelter and stood there rigidly, conscious of the soft bosom and the breath behind it, and the perfume. Her arms and her coat were warm around me. For some reason I thought suddenly and longingly of a boy at home named Raymond Trout, who could walk on his hands, and spit like a man. I remembered his voice in the twilight shouting, "All-ee, all-ee in free!"

"Relax, you little giraffe," Mrs. Fenwick said teasingly. "Really, Howard—" ("Howard! " I thought.) "Your daughter feels just as bony and on guard as a little captured giraffe."

I hated her for that, too; for the first time I felt as Avalon must feel: that I was an unfinished product, ridiculous for this reason, as goslings, half-grown cats, and colts are, having lost their infancy's appeal and not yet having gained the authority of being grown.

So for this, and for calling my father "Howard," I knew at last how much I hated Mrs. Fenwick, and freed myself from her embrace.

"I'd rather go and get my sweater," I said brusquely.

"You'd better go and get in bed if you can't be more polite," my father chided.

But now it was impossible to be polite to Mrs. Fenwick. When she begged me not to chew the stalks of beach grass because she had heard of a child who had died of anthrax from doing this, I skipped before her along the path, pulling stalks and chewing them defiantly. When she invited me to go to the movies I said that movies gave me a headache, and when she offered me candy I said I wasn't hungry. Both lies. Sometimes she brought me presents, and while I accepted them (they were good presents), it was all I could do to thank her.

"She is a lovely person," my father said, and though the words weren't spoken as a question, I knew that he desired an answer, and I gave none.

They were always together, and I tagged along. In the evenings they sat on the veranda long after I had gone to bed. I never heard the typewriter now, as I went off to sleep. Sometimes we would go down to the deserted "ballroom" in the basement where there was a piano. It was afflicted with a seaside twang, but she would play on it and sing in German or English. When she sang in English she pronounced the words as trained singers do; to me they sounded elegant, distorted, and embarrassing. But my father looked as though he could not hear enough, or watch enough.

Summer was nearly over. We were to leave Harbor Landing on the last day of August, while Mrs. Fenwick and her aunt planned to stay through Labor Day. "It will only be a week," she said to my father, and he said: "That week will have too many days in it."

But on the twenty-ninth Mrs. Fenwick had an unexpected visitor: a gentleman who arrived in a white Wills-St. Clair roadster with the top down. He had a red-bronze sunburn, and in the gray hair that rippled back from his forehead there was a glimpse of red-bronze bald spot. His gray mustache was twisted with wax into a little quill at each corner.

"Why, *Carroll!*" cried Mrs. Fenwick, when she saw him. "How on earth—why didn't you let me *know?* You never *said*—"

"I wanted to surprise you! I'm on my way to Bar Harbor"—"Bah Habbah," he called it—"to stop with the Murrays for Labor Day. So I thought, I'll just take a detour"—"daytaw," he called it—"and spend a few days with Meta."

I saw the way his fingers slid up and down the inside of her smooth arm; and I saw her draw the arm away.

"Aren't you glad to see me?"

"Of course, Carroll. Surprised, that's all. You startled me."

I didn't think she cared for her surprise, and when she introduced the man, Mr. Bailey, to my father, it was the first time I had ever seen her look uncomfortable, not in command. My father must have noticed it. I saw his eyes go from her face to Mr. Bailey's and back to hers. After a minute of talking he put his hand on my shoulder.

"Beach time, Sue. Go get your things."

Mrs. Fenwick and her friend were not in the dining room for lunch that day. They were not there for dinner. Alone at the table, Miss Currier picked daintily and ravenously at her food.

My father and I sat in the lounge to play our evening games, and every time someone entered or went past the door he looked up quickly. "Daddy, you're not paying *attention!*" I said. I was winning all the games, but it was not fun to win them this way.

Mr. Bailey did not stay for his "few days" after all. He left early the next morning, and no one saw him off. Calvin the bellboy told me that.

My father had promised, on this last day, to take Avalon and me for a picnic at a lighthouse twenty miles away.

"But isn't Mrs. Fenwick coming?" I asked him.

"No," he said, and slammed the car door firmly.

That day was flawless, and at the end of it Avalon and I had our good-byes. "You write me now, Susie!"

"Oh, I will, and you write me! Promise?"

"I promise."

We knew that we would never write.

As we went in to dinner that night I noticed that though my father smiled and greeted Mrs. Fenwick and her aunt, he did not stop to speak to them as he usually did. I skipped gaily to my place and ate an enormous dinner.

Afterward we had the veranda to ourselves; it was too damp for everyone but us. Fog had come smoking in from the sea, milky, and so dense that it collected on the eaves and dripped from them. Far, far away the harbor buoy tolled on the lifting tide.

"It's the last time," I said mournfully, for though I was not very fond of that veranda I had a superstitious regard for leave-takings. My father did not reply. He smoked in silence, and I forbore to rock my chair.

Behind us the screen door opened, closed. There was a smell of perfume in the air. My father stood up.

"Good evening," he said, severely.

She came and stood before him wearing her blue cashmere coat. She did not need to touch him with her hand; she used her voice.

"Howard," she said. "Howard?"

I understood her tone. It was one I sometimes used myself, pleading for something I wanted very badly. Hoping for something.

"Susie, it's your bedtime," my father said.

I was outraged. "It is *not!*"

"You have packing to do, I think."

"I have *not*. It's done."

Mrs. Fenwick took my hand in hers, a full, smooth hand; I snatched my own away.

"Susie, dear. Honey. Forgive me, will you? I want

to talk to your father, may I? Alone? Just for a little while?"

"Scat, Susie," said my father, and then, more kindly: "I'm sure you have some things to do. We won't be long."

I wasn't a baby. I couldn't howl and clutch the railing. I left without a word. As I went through the lounge I looked back and saw his arm come up around her shoulders.

My father was wrong; I had no "things to do." My suitcase was packed; my traveling clothes were ready. The room was bare and tidy, home no longer, and through the window came the sound of the far bell.

I told myself they wouldn't mind if I went back to the lounge, where there were magazines to read. How could they mind that? Still, I tiptoed as I crossed the varnished floor to the magazine table. The lounge was deserted except for an old man in a chair, asleep and puffing softly.

Fog muffled the town noises, but the bell came clear, and the voices of the two on the veranda were a steady murmur. Hers, then his, then hers again. I turned the pages of a *National Geographic* and studied the pictures of a Dyak family, all with large stomachs.

"No!" said my father loudly from the porch.

Her voice rose, too. "But, Howard, honestly! What

did you think . . . what can you expect? . . . I am not a nun!"

"But *that* fellow . . . how could you *bring* yourself—"

Her voice murmured and murmured, then rose again: "I thought we could be honest with each other. I really did. I thought we *should* be . . ."

"But that fellow. That tin-plate Percy Millionbucks. My God!"

Murmur, murmur, from her; then his voice gruff and abrupt. I had heard voices like these before, in my own house, when they thought I was asleep. Hers came up again.

". . . didn't suppose that you'd be pleased, but this boorish jealousy . . . I never would have imagined, I never would have *dreamed*—"

"Very well. All right. I'm a boor. But there's a name I could call you, too, you know, Meta!"

I heard her gasp, and I knew she stood up suddenly: her rocker banged to and fro with an agitated sound.

"*Enough!*" she cried. "That will be enough!"

Her footsteps came ringing on the boards, and I shrank back as she sailed through the door. Her anger went by me like a ship on fire: I swear I felt its heat.

The rocker on the porch soon stopped its noise. There was the dripping fog, the harbor bell; nothing else. After a while I tiptoed to the door. My father stood with his back to me, staring out at the blank night.

"Daddy?"

He turned on me. "For Christ's *sake,* Susie! What are you doing lurking there! I told you to get to *bed!*" He had never spoken to me in such a tone in all my life, and I began to cry.

"Oh, my God!" he said. "Tears, now! *Tears!*" He left me and strode through the lounge. The old man never stirred.

My father apologized the next morning; he was really sorry and concerned. And he told me that I was not to worry about what I'd heard; that he and Mrs. Fenwick had become very fond of one another, that she had caused him pain and he'd reacted badly—"hurt her feelings," he put it—but that everything would be "all right," because he was going to explain to her and tell her he was sorry.

"Grownups aren't always as grown up as they'd like to be," he said. "Years haven't much to do with it, unfortunately. You'll find that out."

I was finding it out. And everything was not "all right" with Mrs. Fenwick. She would not see my father. She would not speak to him.

"But she'd see *you,* Susie," he said, shameless with anxiety as the morning wore on; we were to leave at noon. "You go see her, you ought to, anyway. Knock on the door and when she hears your voice . . . tell her . . . no, wait, I'll send a note with you."

With his letter in my hand I walked slowly down the stuffy hall and around the corner to her door. Number 33. I knocked on it, then called her name, but there was no answer. I tried the handle; the door was not locked and I opened it gently, planning to leave the letter on her bureau. I was curious, too. I had never seen her room.

She was lying on the bed asleep.

I stood and looked at her. She had taken the pins out of her hair; they lay in a small heap on the bedside table with her earrings and a wrinkled handkerchief. Her hair covered her shoulders in a silky fall. Her eyelashes were dark and long. She slept gracefully, with her mouth closed, and the room was full of her perfume.

I looked at her for a minute, or a second; long enough, anyway, to remember her asleep forever, and then I went out of the room and closed the door as quietly as I could. I tore the letter up and dropped the pieces into one of the red fire buckets that hung on a hook by the stairs. Then I leaned against the wall and waited for my heart to quiet down; it was banging like the rockers on the porch.

When I turned the corner I saw my father waiting in his doorway.

"Did you give it to her, Sue? What did she say?"

"She tore it up," I said. "She never opened it. She just stood there and tore it up."

"Oh," he said, and his face turned dull. "Well, I guess she's . . . well, never mind. Never mind . . . Are you all ready?"

Indeed I was ready, and more than ready.

"Hurry, Daddy, come on, let's go!"

"Yes, all right . . . oh, here's Calvin. These two, Calvin; I'll take the others. . . ." And then as I waited, nervously snapping my hat elastic under my chin, he turned away, turned to the window, and put his hand to his forehead just for a moment as if his head ached, and something about that simple gesture showed me how unhappy he was. I was appalled. I must tell him. Could I tell him? But I thought I could not. I thought I had gone too far, and was afraid.

"Daddy, let's *go!*"

"Yes. All right. Right now."

He didn't even turn his head as we went by her door, and I was perfectly miserable all the way home. I suppose I knew then that by my action I had lost my father just as truly as Mrs. Fenwick had.

THE STATE
OF GRACE

Harold Brodkey

There is a certain shade of red brick—a dark, almost melodious red, sombre and riddled with blue—that is my childhood in St. Louis. Not the real childhood, but the false one that extends from the dawning of consciousness until the day that one leaves home for college. That one shade of red brick and green foliage is St. Louis in the summer (the winter is just a gray sky and a crowded school bus and the wet footprints on the brown linoleum floor at school), and that brick and a pale sky is spring. It's also loneliness and the queer, self-pitying wonder that children whose families are having catastrophes feel.

I can remember that brick best on the back of our apartment house; it was on all the apartment houses on that block, and also on the apartment house where Edward lived—Edward was a small boy I took care of on the evenings when his parents went out. As I came up the street from school, past the boulevard and its ugliness (the vista of shoe-repair shops, dime stores, hairdressers', pet shops, the Tivoli Theatre, and the closed Piggly Wiggly, about to be converted into a Kroger's), past the place where I could see the Masonic Temple, built in the shape of some Egyptian relic, and the two huge concrete pedestals flanking the boulevard (what they supported I can't remember, but on both of them, in brown paint, was a large heart and the information that someone named Erica loved someone named Peter), past the post office, built in W.P.A. days of yellow brick and chrome, I hurried toward the moment when at last, on the other side, past the driveway of the garage of the Castlereagh Apartments, I would be at the place where the trees began, the apartment houses of dark-red brick, and the empty stillness.

In the middle of that stillness and red brick was my neighborhood, the terribly familiar place where I was more comfortably an exile than anywhere else. There were two locust trees that were beautiful to me—I think because they were small and I could encompass them (not only with my mind and heart but with my hands as well). Then came an apartment house of red brick (but not quite the true shade) where a boy I knew lived, and two amazingly handsome brothers, who were also strong and kind, but much older than I and totally uninterested in me. Then came an alley of black macadam and another vista, which I found

shameful but drearily comfortable, of garages and ash-
pits and telephone poles and the backs of apartment
houses—including ours—on one side, the backs of
houses on the other. I knew many people in the apartments but none in the houses, and this was the ulti-
mate proof, of course, to me of how miserably degraded
I was and how far sunken beneath the surface of the
sea. I was on the bottom, looking up through the
waters, through the shifting bands of light—through,
oh, innumerably more complexities than I could stand—
at a sailboat driven by the wind, some boy who had
a family and a home like other people.

I was thirteen, and six feet tall, and I weighed a
hundred and twenty-five pounds. Though I fretted
wildly about my looks (my ears stuck out and my
hair was like wire), I also knew I was attractive; girls
had smiled at me, but none whom I might love and
certainly none of the seven or eight goddesses in the
junior high school I attended. Starting in about second
grade, I always had the highest grades—higher than
anybody who had ever attended the schools I went
to—and I terrified my classmates. What terrified them
was that so far as they could see, it never took any
effort; it was like legerdemain. I was never teased, I
was never tormented; I was merely isolated. But I was
known as "the walking encyclopedia," and the only
way I could deal with this was to withdraw. Looking

back, I'm almost certain I could have had friends if I'd made the right overtures, and that it was not my situation but my forbidding pride that kept them off; I'm not sure. I had very few clothes, and all that I had had been passed to me from an elder cousin. I never was able to wear what the other boys wore.

Our apartment was on the third floor. I usually walked up the back stairs, which were mounted outside the building in a steel framework. I preferred the back stairs—it was a form of rubbing at a hurt to make sure it was still there—because they were steep and ugly and had garbage cans on the landings and wash hanging out, while the front door opened off a court where rosebushes grew, and the front stairs were made of some faintly yellow local marble that was cool and pleasant to the touch and to the eye. When I came to our back door, I would open the screen and call out to see if my mother was home. If she was not home, it usually meant that she was visiting my father, who had been dying in the hospital for four years and would linger two more before he would come to terms with death. As far as I know, that was the only sign of character he ever showed in his entire life, and I suppose it was considerable, but I hoped, and even sometimes prayed, that he would die—not only because I wouldn't have to visit the hospital again, where the white-walled rooms were filled with odors and

sick old men (and a tangible fear that made me feel a
falling away inside, like the plunge into the uncon-
scious when the anesthetic is given), but because my
mother might marry again and make us all rich and
happy once more. She was still lovely then, still alight
with the curious incandescence of physical beauty, and
there was a man who had loved her for twenty years
and who loved her yet and wanted to marry her. I
wished so hard my father would die, but he just
wouldn't. If my mother was home, I braced myself
for unpleasantness, because she didn't like me to sit
and read; she hated me to read. She wanted to drive
me outdoors, where I would become an athlete and
be like other boys and be popular. It filled her with
rage when I ignored her advice and opened a book;
once, she rushed up to me, her face suffused with
anger, took the book (I think it was "Pride and Prej-
udice"), and hurled it out the third-story window. At
the time, I sat and tried to sneer, thinking she was
half mad, with her exaggerated rage, and so foolish
not to realize that I could be none of the things she
thought I ought to be. But now I think—perhaps
wistfully—that she was merely desperate, driven to
extremes in her anxiety to save me. She felt—she
knew, in fact—that there was going to come a moment when, like an acrobat, I would have to climb
on her shoulders and on the shoulders of all the things

she had done for me, and leap out into a life she couldn't imagine (and which I am leading now), and if she wanted to send me out wrapped in platitudes, in an athletic body, with a respect for money, it was because she thought that was the warmest covering.

But when I was thirteen, I only wondered how anyone so lovely could be so impossible. She somehow managed it so that I hated her far more than I loved her, even though in the moments before sleep I would think of her face, letting my memory begin with the curving gentleness of her eyelids and circle through all the subtle interplay of shadows and hollows and bones, and the half-remembered warmth of her chest, and it would seem to me that this vision of her, always standing in half light (as probably I had seen her once when I was younger, and sick, perhaps, though I don't really remember), was only as beautiful to me as the pattern in an immeasurably ancient and faded Persian rug. In the vision, as in the rug, I could trace the lines in and out and experience some unnamed pleasure, but it had almost no meaning, numbed as I was by the problem of being her son.

Being Jewish also disturbed me, because it meant I could never be one of the golden people—the blond athletes, with their easy charm. If my family had been well off, I might have felt otherwise, but I doubt it.

My mother had a cousin whom I called Aunt Rachel,

and we used to go and see her three or four times a year. I hated it. She lived in what was called the Ghetto, which was a section of old houses in downtown St. Louis with tiny front porches and two doors, one to the upstairs and one to the downstairs. Most people lived in them only until they could move to something better; no one had ever liked living there. And because of that, the neighborhood had the quality of being blurred; the grass was never neat, the window frames were never painted, no one cared about or loved the place. It was where the immigrants lived when they arrived by train from New York and before they could move uptown to the apartments near Delmar Boulevard, and eventually to the suburbs—to Clayton, Laclede, and Ladue. Aunt Rachel lived downstairs. Her living room was very small and had dark-yellow wallpaper, which she never changed. She never cleaned it, either, because once I made a mark on it, to see if she would, and she didn't. The furniture was alive and frightening; it was like that part of the nightmare where it gets so bad that you decide to wake up. I always had to sit on it. It bulged in great curves of horsehair and mohair, and it was dark purple and maroon and dark green, and the room had no light in it anywhere. Somewhere on the other side of the old, threadbare satin draperies that had been bought out of an old house was fresh air and sunshine, but you'd never know it. It was as much like a peasant's hut as Aunt Rachel could manage, buying furniture in cut-rate furniture stores. And always there were the smells—the smell of onion soup and garlic and beets. It was the only place where I was ever rude to my mother in public. It was always full of people whom I hardly ever knew, but who knew me, and I had to perform. My mother would say, "Tell the people what your last report card was," or "Recite them the poem that Miss Huntington liked so well." That was when the feeling of unreality was strongest. Looking back now, I think that what frightened me was their fierce urgency; I was to be rich and famous and make all their tribulations worth while. But I didn't want that responsibility. Anyway, if I were going to be what they wanted me to be, and if I had to be what I was, then it was too much to expect me to take them as they were. I had to go beyond them and despise them, but first I had to be with them— and it wasn't fair.

It was as if my eyelids had been propped open, and I had to see these things I didn't want to see. I felt as if I had taken part in something shameful, and there- fore I wasn't a nice person. It was like my first sexual experiences: What if anyone knew? What if everyone found out? . . . How in hell could I ever be gallant and carefree?

The State of Grace

I had read too many books by Englishmen and New Englanders to want to know anything but graceful things and erudite things and the look of white frame houses on green lawns. I could always console myself by thinking my brains would make me famous (brains were good for something, weren't they?), but then my children would have good childhoods—not me. I was irrevocably deprived, and it was the irrevocableness that hurt, that finally drove me away from any sensible adjustment with life to the position that dreams had to come true or there was no point in living at all. If dreams came true, then I would have my childhood in one form or another, someday.

If my mother was home when I came in from school, she might say that Mrs. Leinberg had called and wanted me to baby-sit, and I would be plunged into yet another of the dilemmas of those years. I had to baby-sit to earn money to buy my lunch at school, and there were times, considering the dilemma I faced at the Leinbergs', when I preferred not eating, or eating very little, to baby-sitting. But there wasn't any choice; Mother would have accepted for me, and made Mrs. Leinberg promise not to stay out too late and deprive me of my sleep. She would have a sandwich ready for me to eat, so that I could rush over in time to let Mr. and Mrs. Leinberg go out to dinner. Anyway, I would eat my sandwich reading a book, to get my own back, and then I would set out. As I walked down the back stairs on my way to the Leinbergs', usually swinging on the railings by my arms to build up my muscles, I would think forlornly of what it was to be me, and wish things were otherwise, and I did not understand myself or my loneliness or the cruel deprivation the vista down the alley meant.

There was a short cut across the back yards to the apartment house where the Leinbergs lived, but I always walked by my two locust trees and spent a few moments loving them; so far as I knew, I loved nothing else.

Then I turned right and crossed the street and walked past an apartment house that had been built at right angles to the street, facing a strange declivity that had once been an excavation for still another apartment house, which had never been built, because of the Depression. On the other side of the declivity was a block of three apartment houses, and the third was the Leinbergs'. Every apartment in it had at least eight rooms, and the back staircase was enclosed, and the building had its own garages. All this made it special and expensive, and a landmark in the neighborhood.

Mr. Leinberg was a drug manufacturer and very successful. I thought he was a smart man, but I don't remember him at all well (I never looked at men closely

in those days but always averted my head in shyness
and embarrassment; they might guess how fiercely I
wanted to belong to them) and I could have been
wrong. Certainly the atmosphere then, during the
war years—it was 1943—was that everyone was getting rich; everyone who could work, that is. At any
rate, he was getting rich, and it was only a matter of
time before the Leinbergs moved from that apartment
house to Laclede or Ladue and had a forty-thousand-
dollar house with an acre or so of grounds.

Mrs. Leinberg was very pretty; she was dark, like
my mother, but not as beautiful. For one thing, she
was too small; she was barely five feet tall, and I
towered over her. For another, she was not at all regal.
But her lipstick was never on her teeth, and her dresses
were usually new, and her eyes were kind. (My mother's eyes were incomprehensible; they were dark stages
where dimly seen mob scenes were staged and all one
ever sensed was tumult and drama, and no matter
how long one waited, the lights never went up and
the scene never was explained.) Mrs. Leinberg would
invite me to help myself in the icebox, and then she
would write down the telephone number of the place
where she was going to be. "Keep Edward in the back
of the apartment, where he won't disturb the baby,"
she would tell me. "If the baby does wake up, pick
her up right away. That's very important. I didn't

pick Edward up, and I'll always regret it." She said that every time, even though I could see Edward lurking in the back hallway, waiting for his parents to leave so he could run out and jump on me and our world could come alive again. He would listen, his small face—he was seven—quite blank with hurt and the effort to pierce the hurt with understanding.

Mrs. Leinberg would say, "Call me if she wakes up." And then, placatingly, to her husband, "I'll just come home to put her back to sleep, and then I'll go right back to the party—" Then, to me, "But she almost always sleeps, so don't worry about it."

"Come on, Greta. He knows what to do," Mr. Leinberg would say impatiently.

I always heard contempt in his voice—contempt for his wife, for Edward, and for me. I would be standing by the icebox looking down on the two little married people. Edward's father had a jealous and petulant mouth. "Come on, Greta," it would say impatiently. "We'll be back by eleven," it would say to me.

"Edward goes to bed at nine," Mrs. Leinberg would say, her voice high and birdlike, but tremulous with confusion and vagueness. Then she would be swept out the front door, so much prettily dressed matchwood, in her husband's wake. When the door closed, Edward would come hurtling down the hall and tackle my knees if I was staring after his parents, or, if I was facing him, leap onto my chest and into my arms.

"What shall we play tonight?"

He would ask that and I would have to think. He trembled with excitement, because I could make up games wonderful to him—like his daydreams, in fact. Because he was a child, he trusted me almost totally, and I could do anything with him. I had that power with children until I was in college and began at last to be like other people.

In Edward's bedroom was a large closet; it had a rack for clothes, a washstand, a built-in table, and fifteen or twenty shelves. The table and shelves were crowded with toys and games and sports equipment. I owned a Monopoly board I had inherited from my older sister, an old baseball glove (which was so cheap I never dared use it in front of my classmates, who had real gloves signed by real players), and a collection of postcards. The first time I saw that closet, I practically exploded with pleasure; I took down each of the games and toys and played with them, one after another, with Edward. Edward loved the fact that we never played a game to its conclusion but would leap from game to game after only a few moves, until the leaping became the real game and the atmosphere of laughter the real sport.

It was comfortable for me in the back room, alone

in the apartment with Edward, because at last I was chief; and not only that, I was not being seen. There was no one there who could see through me, or think of what I should be or how I should behave; and I have always been terrified of what people thought of me, as if what they thought was a hulking creature that would confront me if I should turn a wrong corner.

There were no corners. Edward and I would take his toy pistols and stalk each other around the bed. Other times, we were on the bed, the front gun turret of a battleship sailing to battle the Japanese fleet in the Indian Ocean. Edward would close his eyes and roll with pleasure when I went "Boom! Boom! BOOOOM!"

"It's sinking! It's sinking, isn't it?"

"No, stupid. We only hit its funnel. We have to shoot again. Boom, Boom—"

Edward's fingers would press his eyelids in a spasm of ecstasy; his delirious, taut, little boy's body would fall backward on the soft pillows and bounce, and his back would curve; the excited breathy laughter would pour out like so many leaves spilling into spring, so many lilacs thrusting into bloom.

Under the bed, in a foxhole (Edward had a Cub Scout hat and I had his plastic soldier helmet), we turned back the yellow hordes from Guadalcanal. Edward dearly loved to be wounded. "I'm hit!" he'd shriek. "I'm hit!" He'd press his hand against his stomach and writhe on the wooden floor. "They shot me in the guts—"

I didn't approve of his getting wounded so soon, because then the scene was over; both his and my sense of verisimilitude didn't allow someone to be wounded and then get up. I remember how pleased he was when I invented the idea that after he got wounded, he could be someone else; so, when we crawled under the bed, we would decide to be eight or twelve or twenty Marines, ten each to get wounded, killed, or maimed as we saw fit, provided enough survived so that when we crawled out from under the bed we could charge the Japanese position under the dining-room table and leave it strewn with corpses.

Edward was particularly good at the detective game, which was a lot more involved and difficult. In that, we would walk into the kitchen, and I would tell him that we had received a call about a murder. Except when we played Tarzan, we never found it necessary to be characters. However, we always had names. In the detective game, we were usually Sam and Fred. We'd get a call telling us who was murdered, and then we'd go back to the bedroom and examine the corpse and question the suspects. I'd fire questions at an empty chair. Sometimes Edward would get tired of being my sidekick and he'd slip into the chair and be the quaking suspect. Other times, he would prowl around the room on his hands and knees with a magnifying glass while I stormed and shouted at the perpetually shifty suspect: "Where were you, Mrs. Eggnogghead [giggles from Edward], at ten o'clock, when Mr. Eggnogghead [laughter, helpless with pleasure, from Edward] was slain with the cake knife?"

"Hey, Fred! *I found bloodstains.*" Edward's voice would quiver with a creditable imitation of the excitement of radio detectives.

"Bloodstains! Where, Sam? Where? This may be the clue that breaks the case."

Edward could sustain the *commedia dell' arte* for hours if I wanted him to. He was a precocious and delicate little boy, quivering with the malaise of being unloved. When we played, his child's heart would come into its own, and the troubled world where his vague hungers went unfed and mothers and fathers were dim and far away—too far away ever to reach in and touch the sore place and make it heal—would disappear, along with the world where I was not sufficiently muscled or sufficiently gallant to earn my own regard. (What ever had induced my mother to marry that silly man, who'd been unable to hang on to his money? I could remember when we'd had a larger house and I'd been happy; why had she let it get away?) It angered me that Edward's mother had so little love for him and so much for her daughter, and that Edward's father should not appreciate the boy's intelligence— he thought Edward was a queer duck, and effeminate. I could have taught Edward the manly postures. But his father didn't think highly of me: I was only a baby-sitter, and a queer duck too. Why, then, should Edward be more highly regarded by his father than I myself was? I wouldn't love him or explain to him.

That, of course, was my terrible dilemma. His apartment house, though larger than mine, was made of the same dark-red brick, and I wouldn't love him. It was shameful for a boy my age to love a child anyway. And who was Edward? He wasn't as smart as I'd been at his age, or as fierce. At his age, I'd already seen the evil in people's eyes, and I'd begun the construction of my defenses even then. But Edward's family was more prosperous, and the cold winds of insecurity *(Where will the money come from?)* hadn't shredded the dreamy chrysalis of his childhood. He was still immersed in the dim, wet wonder of the folded wings that might open if someone loved him; he still hoped, probably, in a butterfly's unthinking way, for spring and warmth. How the wings ache, folded so, waiting; that is, they ache until they atrophy.

So I was thirteen and Edward was seven and he wanted me to love him, but he was not old enough or strong enough to help me. He could not make his parents share their wealth and comfort with me, or force them to give me a place in their home. He was like most of the people I knew—eager and needful of my love; for I was quite remarkable and made incredible games, which were better than movies or than the heart could hope for. I was a dream come true. I was smart and virtuous (no one knew that I occasionally stole from the dime store) and fairly attractive, maybe even very attractive. I was often funny and always interesting. I had read everything and knew everything and got unbelievable grades. Of course I was someone whose love was desired. Mother, my teachers, my sister, girls at school, other boys—they all wanted me to love them.

But I wanted them to love me first.

None of them did. I was fierce and solitary and acrid, marching off the little mile from school, past the post office, all yellow brick and chrome, and my two locust trees (water, water everywhere and not a drop to drink), and there was no one who loved me first. I could see a hundred cravennesses in the people I knew, a thousand flaws, a million weaknesses. If I had to love first, I would love only perfection. Of course, I could help heal the people I knew if I loved them. No, I said to myself, why should I give them everything when they give me nothing?

How many hurts and shynesses and times of walking up the back stairs had made me that way? I don't know. All I know is that Edward needed my love and I wouldn't give it to him. I was only thirteen. There isn't much you can blame a boy of thirteen for, but I'm not thinking of the blame; I'm thinking of all the years that might have been—if I'd only known then what I know now. The waste, the God-awful waste.

Really, that's all there is to this story. The boy I was, the child Edward was. That and the terrible desire to suddenly turn and run shouting back through the corridors of time, screaming at the boy I was, searching him out, and pounding on his chest: Love him, you damn fool, love him.

SHORT PAPA

James Purdy

W hen I caught a glimpse of Short Papa coming through the back yard that cold sleety February afternoon I had straight away a funny feeling it might be the last time he would visit me. He looked about the same, tall and lean and wind-burned, but despite the way he kept his shoulders back and his head up he spoke and shook hands like a man who didn't expect you to believe a word he said.

Neither Mama nor Sister Ruth budged an inch when I told them who was out on the back porch, but after a struggle with herself, Ma finally said, "You can give Short Papa this plate of hot Brunswick stew, and let him get his strength back from wherever he has been this time. And then you tell him, Lester, he has got to light out again soon as possible."

"But, Ma," I began, "can't he just stay the night?"

"Father or not father," she began, "after what that man has done to us, no. . . . I'll feed him but I won't

121

take him in, and you give him my message, hear? Eat and get!"

But I seen that my remark about how after all it was my own Dad who had come to see me had moved Ma more than a little, for her breast rose and fell like it always does when she is wrought up.

"He'll only get in more trouble if he stays, Lester, and he'll get you in trouble too. I do regret to talk against your Papa, but he is a no-account, low-down . . ."

She stopped, though, when she saw the expression on my face.

Short Papa sat, hands folded, on a little green wicker upright chair before the round green wicker table as I brought him his hot plate of Brunswick stew to the back porch.

"Thank you, Les." He eyed the plate and then took it from me. I can still see the way he ate the fricassee chicken and little bits of lima beans and potatoes. He was most famished.

"You can assure your Ma I'll be on my way right after sunset," he replied to the message I bore from her. "Tell her I don't want folks to see me in town . . . by daylight."

I nodded, looking at his empty plate.

"Your Ma has taken awful good care of you, Les. I observed that right away. I'm grateful to her for that, you can tell her. The day I get back on my feet, son, I will see to it that a lot of the things owin' to you will be yours. . . . Count on me."

I didn't quite know what he meant then, but I was pleased he felt I deserved something. Ma didn't often make me feel deserving.

Short Papa got up from the table, loosened his suspenders under his suit coat, felt in his breast pocket as he kept clearing his throat, and then sat down again as he said, "Matter of fact, Les, I have brought you a little something. But first you best take this plate back to the kitchen, for you know how fussy your Ma is about dirty dishes standing around."

I rushed with the plate back to the kitchen and on the double back to Short Papa, and sat down beside him on a little taboret which we use for sitting on.

"I want you to promise me, though, you won't lose it after I give it to you," Short Papa said solemnly.

I promised.

"Cross your heart and all that." Short Papa sort of grinned, but I knew he was dead serious and wanted me to be.

"Cross my heart, Papa."

"All right, Lester. Then here it is."

He handed me a great, really heavy gold watch with a massive chain a-hanging from it.

"Don't you worry now, Les. It is not stolen. It is

your Great-Grandpa's watch. All during my most recent trouble I kept it in a safety deposit vault over at Moortown. I got behind on the annual rent payments when I was in jail, but the bank trusted me, Les, and they kept it. I have paid up for the arrears and this watch is yours. It has been in the family for well over a hundred years, you can count on that."

I was not really glad to get the watch, and yet I wanted it too. I wanted also to show Short Papa I was grateful, and so I hugged and kissed him. His eyes watered a little and he turned away from me, and then he laughed and slapped my shoulder several times.

"Keep it in a safe place, Les, for beyond what it's worth, which aint inconsiderable, it's your old Pa and his Pa, and his Pa before him that owned it. Understand? 'Course you do. . . ."

After Short Papa left, I sat for a long time on the back porch listening to my watch tick. It had a powerful beat to it. From behind me I could hear Ma talking with Sister Ruth about the dress they were making for her wedding. Ruth was going to be married in June.

I considered how Short Papa's sudden arrival and departure had made no impression on them. He might as well have been the man who comes to collect the old papers and tin cans. Yet he was Ruth's father too.

"You take my word for it, Les, things are going to be hunky-dory one day for all of us again."

That was what Pa had said to me as he slipped out the back way in the gathering darkness, and like the ticking of my watch those words kept pounding in my ears.

Ma had made me ashamed of Papa always reminding me of the many times he had been sent to jail for a short stretch (hence his nickname), and once out, he would only be sent back again, and so on and so forth, but there was now something about the way this watch ticking away in my possession made me feel not only different about Papa and his Pa and his Pa before him, I felt for the first time I was connected with somebody, or with something. I felt I had a basic, you see. But I didn't want anybody to know I had the watch, and I also felt that I would never see Short Papa again, that he had come back, so to speak his piece and be gone for good.

As a result I felt awful crushed that Short Papa had been entertained so miserly by Ma, being fed on the back porch like a tramp, and then dismissed. But then Ma's attitude toward Pa was hard to fathom, for though she never wanted any more to do with him she never

said anything about getting a divorce. She just didn't
want any more men around, for one thing, and then,
as she said, why go to the bother of divorcing somebody when you was already divorced from him for
good and all. . . .

I kept the watch under my pillow at night, and I
wound it cautiously and slow twice a day, like he had
instructed me, and I never let it out of my sight whilst
I was awake, keeping it with me at all times. I could
not imagine being without it ever now.

After a couple to three months of this great care
with his watch, and to tell the truth getting a little
weary sometimes with the worry and guardianship
bestowed on it, the polishing and keeping it when
unused in its own little cotton case, and also seeing it
was hid from Ma, for I feared she might claim it away
from me for what Pa owed her, I remember the time
it happened: It was an unsteady spring afternoon, when
it couldn't make up its mind whether it was still winter
or shirt-sleeves weather, and I had gone to the Regal
Pool Parlors to watch the fellows shoot pool, for at
this time their hard-fast rule there was that nobody
under sixteen was allowed to play, but you could be
a spectator provided you kept your mouth shut.

Absorbed in the games and the talk of the older
fellows, before I was aware of it all the shadows had
lengthened outside and the first street lights had begun

to pop on, and so then almost automatically I began to lift the chain to my watch, and as I did so I was all at once reminded of another time further back when Short Papa had been teaching me to fish and he had said nervously: "Pull up your rod, Les, you've got a bite there!" And I had pulled of course and felt the rod heavy at first and weighted but then pulling harder I got this terrible lightness, and yanking the pole to shore there was nothing on the hook at all, including no bait neither. And pulling now on the watch chain I drew up nothing from my pocket. My watch was gone. I got faint-sick all over. I was too shaky in fact to get up and start looking. I was pretty sure, nonplussed though I was, that I had not lost it here in the Regal Pool Parlors, but I went over to Bud Hughes the manager, who knew me and my family, and told him.

Bud studied my face a long time, and then finally I saw he believed me, but he kept asking a few more questions, like where I had got the watch in the first place, and when. I lied to him then because if he had knowed it come direct from Short Papa he would have thought it was stolen. So I told him the far side of the truth, that it was from my Great-Grandfather, passed on to me, and this seemed to satisfy him, and he said he would be on the lookout.

Almost every day thereafter on the way home from

school I stopped in at the Regal to see if they had any news about my watch, and it got to be a kind of joke there with the customers and with Bud especially. I think they were almost half-glad to see me show up so regular, and inquire.

"No news, though, yet about your great-grandfather's watch," Bud Hughes would generally manage to quip at some time during my visit, and he would wink at me.

Then the joke about the missing watch having run its course, no mention was finally ever made of it again, and then after a while I quit going to the Regal entirely.

I held on to the chain, though, like for dear life, and never left it out of my grasp if I could help it.

During this period of what must have been a year or two, Ma would often study me more carefully than usual as if she had decided there was something wrong somewhere, but then finally decided she didn't want to know maybe what it was, for she had enough other worries nagging away at her.

About this time, school being out, and the long summer vacation getting under way, I got me a job in a concession at Auglaize Amusement Park selling Cracker Jack and candy bars in the arcade that faces the river. They give me a nice white uniform and cap, and for the first time the girls began making eyes at me. . . . I realized that summer I was growing up, and I also realized I would soon be able to leave Ma for good and fend for myself.

On the way to work I would pass this fortune teller's booth early each P.M. and the lady who told the fortunes was usually seated in a silk upholstered armchair outside, and got to know me by sight. She wasn't exactly young or old, and went under the name Madame Amelia. She was also very pleasant to me partly because she knowed I worked in the concession. One time right out of the blue she told me she would be happy to give a nice young boy starting out a free reading but not to wait too long to come in and take advantage of it, now business was still a bit slack.

I had sort of a crush on a young girl who come in now with her soldier boyfriend and bought popcorn from me, and I wanted like everything to find out her name and if she was going to be married to her boyfriend. So I decided finally to take advantage of Madame Amelia's invitation and offer. . . . The fortune telling booth with the smell of incense and jingle of little wind chimes and the perfume of red jasmine which she wore on her own person, the thought of the girl I loved and her soldier friend sort of went right out of my head and vanished into thin air.

I felt an old hurt begin to throb inside me.

Madame Amelia at first sort of flailed around asking

me a few leading questions, such as where I had grown up, if I was the only boy in the family and if I had worked in the concession before, and so on—all just to get her warmed up, as I later found out was the practice with "readers." But then just before she began the actual fortune in earnest, she held her breast, her eyes closed tight, and she looked so tortured and distressed I thought she was about to have a heart attack, but it was all part also of her getting in touch with the "hidden forces" which was to direct her sorting out your fortune.

Then she got very calm and quiet, and looked me straight in the eye.

I stirred under her searching scowl.

"Before I begin, Lester," she said, shading her brow, "I must ask you something, for you are a good subject, my dear—I can tell—and unusually receptive for a young boy. What I would get for you, therefore, would come from deeper down than just any ordinary fortune. Is that clear?"

She looked at me very narrowly. "In other words, Lester, do you want to hear the truth or do you just want the usual amusement park rigmarole?"

"The truth, Madame Amelia," I said as resolutely as I could.

She nodded, and touched my hand.

"You have had two losses, Lester," she began now

at once in a booming voice. "But you know only about one of them, I see."

The words "the truth" seemed to form again and again on my tongue like the first wave of severe nausea.

"As I say," she was going on, "you have lost two things precious to you. A gift, and a man who loves you very deeply.

"The hand that gave you the gift which you have not been able to locate, that hand has been cold a long time, and will soon turn to dust. You will never see him again in this life."

I gave out a short cry, but Madame Amelia pointed an outstretched finger at me which would have silenced a whole auditorium.

"Long since turned to dust," she went on pitilessly. "But the gift which he bestowed on you is not lost." Her voice was now soft and less scary. "I see a bed, Lester, on which you sleep. . . . The gift so precious to both the giver and the receiver you will find within the mattress . . . in a small opening."

I do not even remember leaving Madame Amelia's, or recall working the rest of the afternoon in the popcorn concession. . . . I do know I ran most of the way home.

Mama was giving a big party for her bridge club, and for once she was in a good humor, so she said very little to me as I rushed past upstairs to my bed-room.

Mama always made my bed so good, I hated to take off the hand-sewn coverlet and the immaculate just-changed and ironed sheet, but I had to know if Madame Amelia was telling me the truth. . . . I hoped and prayed she was wrong, that she had lied, and that I would not find the watch, for if that part of the fortune was not true, neither would be the other part about the hand of the bestower.

I searched and searched but could find no little ap-erture where my watch would have slipped down in the mattress, until when about to give up, all at once I see under one of the button-like doohickeys a sort of small opening. . . . My hand delved down, my heart came into my mouth, I felt the cold metal, I pulled it out, it was my gold watch.

But instead of the joy at having it back, I felt as bad as if I had killed somebody. Sitting there with the timepiece which I now wound carefully, I lost all track of my surroundings. I sat there on the unmade bed for I don't know how long, hardly looking at my long-lost friend, which ticked on and on uncomfort-ingly.

"Lester?" I heard Mama's troubled voice. "Why, where on earth did you ever get that beautiful watch?"

I looked up at her, and then I told it all to her. . . .

She looked at the tousled condition of sheets, coverlet, and mattress, but there come from her no crit-
icism or scolding.

She held the watch now in her own palm and gazed
at it carefully but sort of absentmindedly.

"You should have told me, Lester, and not kept it
locked in your own heart all this time. You should
confide in Mama more. Just look at you, too, you're
growing into a handsome young man right in front
of my eyes."

A queer kind of sob escaped from her. . . .

"Where is Short Papa, do you suppose?" I got out
at last as she took my hand.

Mama smoothed my hair briefly, then she went on:

"I have wondered and wondered how I was to tell
you all these months, Lester, and I see that as usual I
must have did the wrong thing where you and Short
Papa are concerned. But you realize I learned of his
death weeks after the event. . . . And then weeks and
weeks after that I heard he had been buried in accord
with his firm instructions that there was to be no
funeral and nobody was to be notified back here of
his passing. . . ."

I nodded, meaning I did not blame her, but kept
looking hard at the watch, and thinking there could
be no place safe enough now for it, and that it must
never part from me again.

"I've always wanted to do what was best, Lester," Mama went on, "but parents too are only after all flesh and blood as someday you will find out for yourself."

She dried her eyes on her tea apron and then touched me softly on the cheek and started to make up the bed, and at the very last to make a final touch she got out her old-fashioned bedspread from the cedar chest and put that over the rayon coverlet.

THE VISITOR

Elizabeth Bowen

Roger was awakened early that morning by the unfamiliar sound of trees in the Miss Emerys' garden. It was these that had made the room so dark the previous evening, obscuring the familiar town lights that shone against the wall above his bed at home, making him feel distant and magnificently isolated in the Miss Emerys' spare room. Now, as the sky grew pale with sunless morning, the ceiling was very faintly netted over with shadows, and when the sun washed momentarily over the garden these shadows became distinct and powerful, obstructive; and Roger felt as though he were a young calf being driven to market netted down in a cart. He rolled over on his back luxuriously, and lay imagining this.

But the imagination game palled upon him earlier than usual, defeated by his returning consciousness of the room. Here was he alone, enisled with tragedy. The thing had crouched beside his bed all night; he had been conscious of it through the thin texture of

137

his dreams. He reached out again now, timidly, ir-resistibly to touch it, and found that it had slipped away, withdrawn into ambush, leaving with him nothing of itself, scarcely even a memory.

He had never slept before in anybody's spare room; theirs at home had been wonderful to him: a port, an archway, an impersonal room with no smell, nothing of its own but furniture, infinitely modifiable by the personality of brushes and sponge-bags, the attitude of shoe-trees, the gesture of a sprawling dress across a chair.

The Miss Emerys' spare room had long serious curtains that hung down ungirt beside the window, fluted into shadows. One never touched the curtains; if one wanted to make the room dark, one drew a blind that had a lace edge and was stamped all over with a pattern of oak leaves. Miss Emery, when she brought Roger up to bed last night, tried to do this, laid one hand on the acorn of the blind cord, but Roger prayed her to desist and she desisted. She understood that one liked to see the sky from bed. She was a sympathetic woman, and made Roger increasingly sorry for all the things he used to think about her blouses.

The furniture was all made of yellow wood, so shiny and one knew so yielding, that one longed to stab and dint it. There were woollen mats that Miss

Dora Emery had made—she had even promised to teach Roger. She had promised this last night, while Roger sat beside her in a drawing room that positively rocked and shimmered in a blinding glare of gaslight. A half-finished rug lay across her knee and rolled and slid noiselessly on the floor when she moved; the woolly, half-animate thing filled Roger with a vague repulsion. "I'm doing the black border now," she had explained, tweaking the clipped strands through the canvas with a crochet hook and knotting them with a flick of her wrist. "Soon I'll be coming to the green part, the pattern, and I shall work in some touches of vermilion. You really must watch then, Roger, it will be so pretty, you'll really be amused." Roger wondered if she would have come to the vermilion, even to the green, by the time his mother died. Miss Emery was not a quick worker. "How much more black will there be before the pattern?" he inquired. "Three inches," said Miss Emery, and he measured out the distance with his finger.

There were paintings on the spare-room wall of moors with Scotch cattle, and over the chest of drawers there was a smaller picture in a green-and-gold frame called "Enfin—Seuls." French. It depicted a lady and gentleman holding each other close and kissing in a drawing room full of palms; they seemed to be glad of something. The paper had a pattern on it,

although Roger's father and mother had said that patterned wallpapers were atrocious. Roger looked at it,
and jumped with his mind from clump to clump—
they were like islands of daisies—pretending he was
a frog who had been given a chance of just eight jumps
to get away from a dragon.

A clock ticked out in the passage; it must be a very
big one, perhaps a stationmaster's clock, given the
Miss Emerys by a relation. It had no expression in its
voice; it neither urged one on nor restrained one, simply commented quite impartially upon the flight of
time. Sixty of these ticks went to make a minute,
neither more nor less than sixty, and the hands of the
clock would be pointing to an hour and a minute when
they came to tell Roger what he was expecting to
hear. Round and round they were moving, waiting
for that hour to come. Roger was flooded by a desire
to look at the face of the clock, and still hearing no
one stirring in the house he crept across to the door,
opened it a crack, quite noiselessly, and looking down
the passage saw that the clock had exactly the same
expression, or absence of expression, as he had imagined. Beyond the clock, a rich curtain of crimson
velvet hung over the archway to the stairs, and a door
painted pale blue stood open a little, showing the
bathroom floor.

Roger had never believed that the Miss Emerys or

any of the people he and his mother visited really went
on existing after one had said good-bye to them and
turned one's back. He had never expressed this disbe-
lief to his mother, but he took it to be an understood
thing, shared between them. He knew, of course,
with his *brain,* that the Miss Emerys (as all the other
people in the roads round them) went on like their
clocks, round and round, talking and eating and washing and saying their prayers; but he didn't *believe* it.
They were, rather, all rolled up swiftly and silently
after one's departure and put away for another occasion, and if one could jump round suddenly, taking
God by surprise, one would certainly find them gone.
If one met a Miss Emery on one's walks, one assumed
she must have sprung up somewhere just out of sight,
like a mushroom, and that after one had passed her,
nothingness would swing down to hide her like a
curtain. Roger *knew* that all the doors round the Miss
Emerys' landing opened on to rooms, or would do
so if he walked through them when he was expected.
But if he opened a door when he was not expected,
would there be anything beyond it but the emptiness
and lightness of the sky? Perhaps even the sky would
not be there. He remembered the fairy tale of Curdie.

The spare room opened off a very private little
corridor that had no other door along it but the bathroom's. The Miss Emerys could not fully have real-

ized the charm of this, or they would have taken the room for their own. Roger had an imaginary house that, when it was quite complete in his mind, he was some day going to live in: in this there were a hundred corridors raying off from a fountain in the centre; at the end of each there was a room looking out into a private garden. The walls of the gardens were so high and smooth that no one could climb over into any-body else's. When they wanted to meet, they would come and bathe together in the fountain. One of the rooms was for his mother, another for his friend Paul. There were ninety-seven still unappropriated, and now it seemed there would be ninety-eight.

Somebody in a room below pulled a blind up with a rush, and began to sweep a carpet. Day was begin-ning in a new house.

The Miss Emerys' breakfast room was lovely. By the window, they had a canary in a cage, that sprang from perch to perch with a wiry, even sound. Out-side, the little early-morning wind had died; the trees were silent, their leaves very still. Since there was no sun this morning, the breakfast table held without competition all the brightness, to radiate it out into the room. No sun could have been rounder or more luminous than the brass kettle genially ridiculous upon a tripod, a blue flame trembling beneath it. There were

dahlias, pink and crimson, and marmalade in a glass
pot shaped like a barrel cast a shadow of gold on the
tablecloth. There was a monstrous tea cosy, its frill
peaked intelligently; and Miss Emery smiled at Roger
over the top of it. There were parrots printed on the
cosy—they battled with one another—so brilliant one
could almost hear them screech. Could a world hold
death that held that cosy? Miss Emery had pinned a
plaid bow tie into the front of her collar. Could she
have done this if what Roger expected must soon
happen to Roger? Must it happen, mightn't it be a
dream?

"Come in, dear," said Miss Emery, while he re-
volved this on the threshold, and Miss Dora Emery,
who had not come to help him to dress (perhaps she
was not allowed to), forced a lump of sugar quickly
between the bars of the canary's cage, and came round
the table to greet him. Roger eyed her cheek uncertainly; it was pink as a peach, and against the light its
curve showed downy: he wondered what was expected of him. They eyed one another with a fleeting
embarrassment, then Miss Dora jerked away a chair
from the table, said "And you sit there, in Claude's
place," and pushed back the chair with him on it,
pausing over him for a second to straighten a knife
beside his plate.

On the table, the hosts of breakfast were marshaled

into two opposing forces, and a Miss Emery from either end commanded each. The toast, eggs, bacon, and marmalade had declared for Miss Dora; but the teapot and its vassals, the cruet and the honeycomb— beautifully bleeding in flowered dish—were for Miss Emery to a man. The loaf, sitting opposite to Roger, remained unabashedly neutral. Roger looked from one Miss Emery to the other.

"Plenty of milk? I expect so; Claude always liked plenty of milk in his tea. What I always say is—little boys like what's good for them, don't you worry, grown-ups!"

"Two pieces of bacon? Look, if this egg's too soft, mop it up with your bread; I should. They *say* it isn't polite, but—"

"Yes, please," said Roger, and "thank you very much, I will." What jolly ladies the Miss Emerys were!

They were looking at him anxiously; were they afraid he was not quite pleased and comfortable? Perhaps they did not often have a visitor. They were aunts; they had once had a nephew called Claude, but he had grown up and gone to India, leaving only some fishing tackle behind him and a book about trains which had been given to Roger. Were they looking piteously at him in the pangs of baffled aunthood? But were they perhaps wondering if he *knew,* how much he knew, and whether they ought to tell him? They were ladies with bright eyes that would fill up easily with emotion, white, quick hands and big bosoms. Roger could hear them saying, "Little motherless boy, poor little motherless boy!" and they would snatch him and gather him in, and each successively would press his head deep into her bosom, so deep that perhaps it would never come out again.

Roger shrank into himself in fearful anticipation: he must escape, he must escape. . . . Yesterday had been one long intrigue for solitude, telling a fib and slipping away from his little sisters, telling a fib and slipping away from his father. Father didn't go to work now but walked about the house and garden, his pink face horribly crinkled up and foolish-looking, lighting cigarettes and throwing them away again. Sometimes he would search anxiously for the cigarette he had thrown away, and when he had picked it up would look at it and sigh desolately to find it had gone quite out. Father was an architect: he would go into his study, tweak a drawing out of a portfolio, run to his desk with it, pore over it, score it through; then start, look back at the door guiltily, return to stare and stare at the drawing, push it away, and go on walking about. Up and down the room he'd go, up and down the room, then dart sideways as though at a sudden loophole and disappear through the door into the garden. But he always came back again to where Roger was; he couldn't let one alone. His presence was a torment and an outrage. Roger disliked people who were ridiculous, and he had never cared to look long at his father. Father had dark-brown hair, all fluffy like a baby's, that stood out away from his head. His face was pink and always a little curly, his eyebrows thick and so far away from his eyes that when one came to them one had forgotten they ought to be there. Lois and Pamela loved him; they thought he was beautiful, so it was all quite fair; and Roger thought *she* was wonderful, the way she had always tolerated him and allowed him to kiss her. Always the best hour of the day for her and Roger had been when the little girls had gone to bed, and *he* had not yet come in. Now the pink face was curled up tight, and the eyes were scared and horrible, and the hands always reaching out to Roger to grab him with "Come on, old man, let's talk. Let's talk for a bit." And they had nothing to say, nothing. And at any moment this man who had no decency might begin talking about *her*.

Now, suppose the Miss Emerys were beginning to—no, the thing was unthinkable. And besides, perhaps they didn't even know.

"What's Roger going to do today?" Miss Emery asked her sister.

"We-ell," said Miss Dora, considering. "He could help you garden, couldn't he? You know you wanted somebody to help you sort the apples. You know you were saying only yesterday, *'If only I had somebody to help me sort the apples!'* Now I wonder if Roger likes sorting apples?"

"Well, I never have," said Roger, "but I expect it would be very nice."

"Yes, you'd love it," said the Miss Emerys with enthusiasm. "Claude loved it, didn't he, Doodsie?" added Miss Dora. "Do you remember how he used to follow you about at all times of the year, even in March and April, saying, 'Aunt Doodsie, mightn't I help you sort the apples?' How I did tease him: I used to say, 'Now then, Mister, I know what you're after! Is it the sorting, or the apples?' Claude was very fond of apples," said Miss Dora, very earnest and explanatory, "he liked apples very much. I expect you do too?"

"Yes, very much, thank you."

"Do you look forward to going back to school?" asked Miss Emery, and her voice knew it was saying something dangerous. Back to school. . . . When mother had died, Father would send him away to school with all the other ugly little boys with round caps. Father said it was the best time of one's life; Father had liked school, he had been that kind of little boy. School *now* meant a day school, where one painted flowers and mothers came rustling in and stood behind one and admired. They had a headmistress, though they were more than half of them little boys, and there were three older than Roger. Father said this wasn't the sort of school for a grown man of nine. This was because Father didn't like the headmistress; she despised him and he grew fidgety in her presence.

"Which school?" said Roger disconcertingly, when he had swallowed his mouthful of bread and honey.

"We-ell," hesitated Miss Dora, "the one you're at now, of course," she said, gathering speed. "It seems to me a very nice school; I like to see you going out to games; and that nice girl behind you with the red hair."

"Yes," said Roger, "that's Miss Williams." He masticated silently, reflecting. Then he said provocatively, "I should like to stay there always."

"O-oh!" deprecated Miss Dora, "but not with little girls. When you're a bigger boy you'll think little girls are silly; you won't want to play with little girls. Claude didn't like little girls."

"How long *do* you think I'll stay?" asked Roger, and watched her narrowly.

"As long as your father thinks well, I expect," said Miss Dora, brightly evasive—"Doodsie, do call poor

Bingo in—or shall I?—and give him his brekky. I can hear him out in the hall."

Roger ignored the liver-colored spaniel that made a waddling entrance and stood beside him, sniffing his bare knees.

"*Why* my father?" he pressed on, raising his eyebrows aggressively at Miss Dora.

"—Bingo-Bingo-Bingo-Bingo-*Bingo!*" cried Miss Dora suddenly, as in convulsive desperation, clapping her hands against her thighs. The spaniel took no notice of her; it twitched one ear, left Roger, and lumbered over to the fireplace, where it sat and yawned into the empty grate.

Roger spent the morning with Miss Emery, helping her sort the apples and range them round in rows along the shelves of the apple room, their cheeks carefully just not touching. The apple room was warm, umber, and nutty-smelling; it had no window, so the door stood open to the orchard, and let in a white panel of daylight with an apple tree in it, a fork impaled in the earth, and a garden hat of Miss Dora's hanging on the end of the fork, tilted coquettishly. The day was white, there were no shadows, there was no wind, never a sound. Miss Emery, her sleeves rolled up, came in and out with baskets of apples that were too heavy for a little boy to carry. Roger, squat-

149

ting on the ground, looked them over for bruises—
a bruised apple would go bad, she said, and must be
eaten at once—and passed up to her those that were
green and perfect, to take their place among the ranks
along the shelves. . . . "That happy throng" . . . It
was like the Day of Judgment, and the shelves were
Heaven. Hell was the hamper in the musty-smelling
corner full of bass matting, where Roger put the Goats.
He put them there reluctantly, and saw himself a kind
angel, with an imploring face turned back to the Im-
placable, driving reluctantly the piteous herd below.

The apples were chilly; they had a blue bloom on
them, and were as smooth as ivory—like dead faces
are, in books, when people bend to kiss them. "They're
cooking apples," said Miss Emery, "not sweet at all,
so I won't offer you one to eat. When we've finished,
you shall have a russet."

"I'd rather, if I might," said Roger, "just bite one
of these. Just bite it."

"Well, bite then," said Miss Emery. "Only don't
take a big one; that would be only waste, for you
won't like it."

Roger bit. The delicate bitter juice frothed out like
milk; he pressed his teeth deep into the resisting white-
ness till his jaws were stretched. Then in the attentive
silence of the orchard he heard steps beginning, coming from the house. Not here, O God, not here! Not

trapped in here among Miss Emery and the apples, when all he wanted when *that* came was to be alone with the clock. If it were here he would hate apples, and he would hate to have to hate them. He looked round despairingly at their green demi-lunes of faces peering at him over the edge of the shelves. His teeth met in his apple, and he bit away such a stupendous mouthful that he was sealed up terrifyingly. The fruit slipped from his fingers and bumped away across the floor. Not a bird or a tree spoke; Miss Emery, standing up behind him on a chair, was almost moveless— listening? The steps came slowly, weighted down with ruefulness. Something to hold on to, something to grip! . . . There was nothing, not even the apple. The door was darkened.

"The butcher *did* come, Miss. Are there any orders?"

But that settled it—the apples were intolerable. Roger asked if he might go now and play in the garden. "Tired?" said Miss Emery, disappointed. "Why, you get tired sooner than Claude—he could go on at this all day. I'm afraid that apple disappointed you. Take a russet, dearie, look, off that corner shelf!"

She was kind; he had no heart to leave behind the russet. So he took it, and walked away among the trees of the orchard, underneath the browning leaves. One slid down through the air and clung against the wool of Roger's jersey; a bronze leaf with blue sheen on it, curled into a tired line. Autumn was the time of the death of the year, but he loved it, he loved the smell of autumn. He wondered if one died more easily then. He had often wondered about death; he had felt in *her* the same curiosity; they had peered down strangely together, as into a bear pit, at something which could never touch them. She was older; she ought to have known, she ought to have known. . . .

The grass was long and lusterless; it let his feet pass through reluctantly. Suppose it wove itself around them, grew into them and held them—somebody's snare. He began the imagination game.

Miss Dora was leaning over the gate talking to some ladies; a mother and daughter, pink, and yet somehow hungry-looking. They turned their heads at the sound of his footsteps in the grass; he dropped his eyes and pretended not to see them. They drank him in, their voices dropped, their heads went closer together. He walked past them through the trees, consciously visible, oh, every line of him conscious—this was how a little boy walked while his mother was dying. . . . Yes, they had been great companions, always together. Yes, she was to die at any moment—poor little boy, wouldn't it be terrible for him! . . . He turned and walked directly away from them, towards the house. Their observation licked his back like flames. Then he hated himself: he did like being looked at.

After lunch, Miss Dora took him down to the High Street with her to buy wool. His mouth was still sleek with apple dumpling, his stomach heavy with it, though they had given him a magazine with horses in it, and sent him off for half an hour to digest. Now they walked by a back way; Miss Dora didn't want to meet people. Perhaps it was awkward for her being seen about with a little boy who half had a mother and half hadn't.

She walked and talked quickly, her hands in a muff; a feather nodded at him over the edge of her hat, the leaves rustled round her feet. He wasn't going to remember last autumn, the way the leaves had rustled . . . running races, catching each other up. He barred his mind against it, and bit his lip till he was quite sick. He wouldn't remember *coming in to tea*— not that.

"What's the matter, darling," said Miss Dora, stopping short concernedly. "Do you want to go somewhere? Have you got a pain?"

"No, oh no," said Roger. "I was just imagining those white mice. How awful losing them, how awful. Do go on about them, Miss Dora, go on about Claude."

153

"—And when he was packing up to go back to school, *there* was the little nest, at the bottom of his playbox, and the little mother mouse, curled up, and Claude said . . ." Miss Dora continued the Saga.

When they got to the town they saw far down at the other end of the High Street the two scarlet tam-o'-shanters of Lois and Pamela, bobbing along beside the lady who had taken *them*. Somebody had given Lois a new hoop; she was carrying it. Pamela was skipping on and off the kerb, in and out of the gutter. She didn't look as if she minded about Mother a bit. Pamela was so young; she was six. He wanted to go and tell Pamela that what she was doing was wrong and horrible, that people must be looking at her out of all the windows of the High Street, and wondering how she could.

"There are the little *sisters,* Roger—rrrrun!"

People would all say, "There are those poor little children, meeting one another!" and tell each other in whispers, behind the windows of the High Street, what was going to happen. He didn't want to be seen talking to his sisters, a little pitiful group.

"Go—on, rrrrun!"

He hung back. He said he would go round and see them after tea, he thought. "Shy of Mrs. Biddle?" asked Miss Dora swiftly. He allowed her to assume it. "Well, of course she *is* a little . . . I mean she isn't quite . . ." said Miss Dora. "But I expect the little girls like her. And I didn't think you were a shy little boy."

Back at the Miss Emerys' by half-past three, Roger found that it was not tea time, and that there was nothing to do, nothing to escape to. That walk with Miss Dora had shattered the imagination game; it wouldn't come back to him till tomorrow, not perhaps for two days. He leaned against an apple tree, and tried sickly to imagine Claude. A horrid little boy, a dreadful little boy; he would have pulled Roger's hair and chaffed him about playing with his mother. Mercifully, he had passed on irrecoverably into the middle years; he was grown up now and would smile down on Roger through the mists of Olympus. Roger didn't get on with other little boys, he didn't like them; they seemed to him like his father, noisy outside and frightened in. Bullies. The school he was going to would be full of these little boys. He wondered how soon he would go to school; perhaps his father was even now writing to the schoolmaster—while Mother lay upstairs with her eyes shut, not caring. Roger thought Father would find this difficult; he smiled at the thought in leisurely appreciation. "Dear Mr. Somebody-or-other, my wife is not dead yet, but she soon will be, and when she is I should like to send

my little boy to your school. . . . If it is not too expensive; I am not a rich man." Roger's father often
said, "I am not a rich man," with an air of modest
complacency.

Home was not so far away from Roger as he stood
in the Miss Emerys' garden. It was twenty minutes
round by the road; from the top of an apple tree one
should be able to see the tall white chimneys. There
had been something wonderful—once—about those
chimneys, standing up against the distant beech trees,
dimming the beech trees, on a quiet evening, with
their pale, unstirring smoke. From up high, here, one
would be able to see the windows of the attics; see
whether the windows were black and open, or whether
the white blinds were down. If he sat from now on,
high in an apple tree, he could watch those windows.
Night and day, nothing should escape him. When the
blinds came down gently and finally to cover them,
Roger would know. There would be no need to tell
him, he would be armored against that. Then he could
run upstairs to the Miss Emerys' landing, and be alone
with the clock. When they came up after him, puffed
with a deep-drawn breath to impart *that,* he could just
turn round and say calmly, rather tiredly, "Oh, it's
all right, thank you, I do know." Then they would
look mortified and go away. Really-kind Miss Emery,

really-kind Father *would* look mortified; they wouldn't like having the thing snatched away from them.

Roger gazed up into the apple tree. The branches were big and far apart, the bark looked slippery. "I'm afraid," he thought, and tried to drown it. He was a little boy, he was afraid of the pain of death. "I don't dare go up, and I don't dare go back to the house. I *must* know, I can't let them tell me. Oh, help me, let them not have to come and tell me! It would be as though they saw me see her being killed. Let it not have to be!"

And now it would be and it must be, even while he deliberated and feared. Roger saw his father open the gate of the orchard and stand hesitatingly, looking round at the trees. He was hatless, his face was puckered up and scared—Oh, to run, to run quickly to somebody who would not know, who would think his mother was still alive, who need never know she was not! To be with somebody comfortable and ignorant, to grasp a cork handle through which this heat couldn't come blazing at him. Horrible footsteps, horrible grey figure coming forward again, and now pausing again desolately among the trees. "Roger?" called the voice, "Roger!"

Roger pressed back. He too was grey like the tree trunks, and slimmer than they; he urged himself against one, hopelessly feigning invisibility, trying to melt. "Roger!" came the voice continuously and wearily, "Old man? Roger!"

Now he was coming straight towards one, he couldn't fail to see. He would drink one in and see one defenseless, and draw a big breath and say IT. No Miss Emery, no cook, no death, no refuge, and the tree shrinking away from before one.

"*Ah, Roger!*"

He thrust his fingers into his ears. "I *know,* I *know!*" he screamed. "Go away, I can't bear it. I know, I tell you."

The pink face lengthened, the scared eyes of his father regarded him, as he stood there screaming like a maniac. A voice was raised, did battle with the din he made, and was defeated. Roger leaned with his arms flung round the girth of the apple tree, grinding his forehead into the bark, clamoring through the orchard. When his own voice dropped he heard how silent it was. So silent that he thought his father was dead too, lying in the long grass, till he turned and saw him beside him, holding something towards him, still standing.

He was holding out a picture postcard; he meant Roger to take it. "Steady, old man," he was saying; "steady, Roger, you're all jiggy: steady, old man!"

"What, what, what?" said Roger, staring wildly at

the postcard. It was glazed and very blue; blue sea, infinitely smooth and distant, sky cloudless above it; white houses gathered joyously together by the shore, other white houses hurrying from the hills. Behind the land, behind everything, the clear fine line of a mountain went up into the sky. Something beckoned Roger; he stood looking through an archway.

"It came for you," said Father, "it's from Aunt Nellie; it's the Bay of Naples."

Then he went away.

This was the blue empty place, Heaven, that one came out into at last, beyond everything. In the blue windlessness, the harmony of that timeless day, Roger went springing and singing up the mountain to look for his mother. He did not think again of that grey figure, frightened, foolish, desolate, that went back among the trees uncertainly, and stood a long time fumbling with the gate.

TOO
EARLY SPRING

Stephen Vincent Benét

I'm writing this down because I don't ever want to forget the way it was. It doesn't seem as if I could, now, but they all tell you things change. And I guess they're right. Older people must have forgotten or they couldn't be the way they are. And that goes for even the best ones, like Dad and Mr. Grant. They try to understand but they don't seem to know how. And the others make you feel dirty or else they make you feel like a goof. Till, pretty soon, you begin to forget yourself—you begin to think, "Well, maybe they're right and it was that way." And that's the end of everything. So I've got to write this down. Because they smashed it forever—but it wasn't the way they said.

Mr. Grant always says in comp. class: "Begin at the beginning." Only I don't know quite where the beginning was. We had a good summer at Big Lake but it was just the same summer. I worked pretty hard at the practice basket I rigged up in the barn, and I learned how to do the back jackknife. I'll never dive like Kerry but you want to be as all-around as you can. And, when I took my measurements, at the end of the summer, I was 5 ft. 9¾ and I'd gained 12 lbs. 6 oz. That isn't bad for going on sixteen and the old chest expansion was O.K. You don't want to get too heavy, because basketball's a fast game, but the year before was the year when I got my height, and I was so skinny, I got tired. But this year, Kerry helped me practice, a couple of times, and he seemed to think I had a good chance for the team. So I felt pretty set up—they'd never had a Sophomore on it before. And Kerry's a natural athlete, so that means a lot for him. He's a pretty good brother too. Most Juniors at State wouldn't bother with a fellow in High.

It sounds as if I were trying to run away from what I have to write down, but I'm not. I want to remember that summer, too, because it's the last happy one I'll ever have. Oh, when I'm an old man—thirty or forty—things may be all right again. But that's a long time to wait and it won't be the same.

And yet, that summer was different, too, in a way. So it must have started then, though I didn't know it. I went around with the gang as usual and we had a good time. But, every now and then, it would strike me we were acting like awful kids. They thought I was getting the big head, but I wasn't. It just wasn't much fun—even going to the cave. It was like going on shooting marbles when you're in High.

I had sense enough not to try to tag after Kerry and his crowd. You can't do that. But when they all got out on the lake in canoes, warm evenings, and somebody brought a phonograph along, I used to go down to the Point, all by myself, and listen and listen. Maybe they'd be talking or maybe they'd be singing, but it all sounded mysterious across the water. I wasn't trying to hear what they said, you know. That's the kind of thing Tot Pickens does. I'd just listen, with my arms around my knees—and somehow it would hurt me to listen—and yet I'd rather do that than be with the gang.

I was sitting under the four pines, one night, right down by the edge of the water. There was a big moon and they were singing. It's funny how you can be unhappy and nobody know it but yourself.

I was thinking about Sheila Coe. She's Kerry's girl. They fight but they get along. She's awfully pretty and she can swim like a fool. Once Kerry sent me over with her tennis racket and we had quite a conversation. She was fine. And she didn't pull any of this big sister stuff, either, the way some girls will with a fellow's kid brother.

And when the canoe came along, by the edge of the lake, I thought for a moment it was her. I thought maybe she was looking for Kerry and maybe she'd

stop and maybe she'd feel like talking to me again. I
don't know why I thought that—I didn't have any
reason. Then I saw it was just the Sharon kid, with
a new kind of bob that made her look grown-up, and
I felt sore. She didn't have any business out on the
lake at her age. She was just a Sophomore in High,
the same as me.

I chunked a stone in the water and it splashed right
by the canoe, but she didn't squeal. She just said,
"Fish," and chuckled. It struck me it was a kid's trick,
trying to scare a kid.

"Hello, Helen," I said. "Where did you swipe the
gunboat?"

"They don't know I've got it," she said. "Oh, hello,
Chuck Peters. How's Big Lake?"

"All right," I said. "How was camp?"

"It was peachy," she said. "We had a peachy counselor, Miss Morgan. She was on the Wellesley field-
hockey team."

"Well," I said, "we missed your society." Of course
we hadn't, because they're across the lake and don't
swim at our raft. But you ought to be polite.

"Thanks," she said. "Did you do the special reading
for English? I thought it was dumb."

"It's always dumb," I said. "What canoe is that?"

"It's the old one," she said. "I'm not supposed to

have it out at night. But you won't tell anybody, will you?"

"Be your age," I said. I felt generous. "I'll paddle awhile, if you want," I said.

"All right," she said, so she brought it in and I got aboard. She went back in the bow and I took the paddle. I'm not strong on carting kids around, as a rule. But it was better than sitting there by myself.

"Where do you want to go?" I said.

"Oh, back towards the house," she said in a shy kind of voice. "I ought to, really. I just wanted to hear the singing."

"K.O.," I said. I didn't paddle fast, just let her slip. There was a lot of moon on the water. We kept around the edge so they wouldn't notice us. The singing sounded as if it came from a different country, a long way off.

She was a sensible kid, she didn't ask fool questions or giggle about nothing at all. Even when we went by Petters' Cove. That's where the lads from the bungalow colony go and it's pretty well populated on a warm night. You can hear them talking in low voices and now and then a laugh. Once Tot Pickens and a gang went over there with a flashlight, and a big Bohunk chased them for half a mile.

I felt funny, going by there with her. But I said,

"Well, it's certainly Old Home Week"—in an offhand tone, because, after all, you've got to be sophisticated. And she said, "People are funny," in just the right sort of way. I took quite a shine to her after that and we talked. The Sharons have only been in town three years and somehow I'd never really noticed her before. Mrs. Sharon's awfully good-looking but she and Mr. Sharon fight. That's hard on a kid. And she was a quiet kid. She had a small kind of face and her eyes were sort of like a kitten's. You could see she got a great kick out of pretending to be grown-up—and yet it wasn't all pretending. A couple of times, I felt just as if I were talking to Sheila Coe. Only more comfortable, because, after all, we were the same age.

Do you know, after we put the canoe up, I walked all the way back home, around the lake? And most of the way, I ran. I felt swell too. I felt as if I could run forever and not stop. It was like finding something. I hadn't imagined anybody could ever feel the way I did about some things. And here was another person, even if it was a girl.

Kerry's door was open when I went by and he stuck his head out, and grinned.

"Well, kid," he said. "Stepping out?"

"Sure. With Greta Garbo," I said, and grinned back to show I didn't mean it. I felt sort of lightheaded, with the run and everything.

"Look here, kid—" he said, as if he was going to say something. Then he stopped. But there was a funny look on his face.

And yet I didn't see her again till we were both back in High. Mr. Sharon's uncle died, back East, and they closed the cottage suddenly. But all the rest of the time at Big Lake, I kept remembering that night and her little face. If I'd seen her in daylight, first, it might have been different. No, it wouldn't have been.

All the same, I wasn't even thinking of her when we bumped into each other, the first day of school. It was raining and she had on a green slicker and her hair was curly under her hat. We grinned and said hello and had to run. But something happened to us, I guess.

I'll say this now—it wasn't like Tot Pickens and Mabel Palmer. It wasn't like Junior David and Betty Page—though they've been going together ever since kindergarten. It wasn't like any of those things. We didn't get sticky and sloppy. It wasn't like going with a girl.

Gosh, there'd be days and days when we'd hardly see each other, except in class. I had basketball practice almost every afternoon and sometimes evenings and she was taking music lessons four times a week. But you don't have to be always twos-ing with a person, if you feel that way about them. You seem to know the way they're thinking and feeling, the way you know yourself.

Now let me describe her. She had that little face and the eyes like a kitten's. When it rained, her hair curled all over the back of her neck. Her hair was yellow. She wasn't a tall girl but she wasn't chunky— just light and well made and quick. She was awfully alive without being nervous—she never bit her fingernails or chewed the end of her pencil, but she'd answer quicker than anyone in the class. Nearly everybody liked her, but she wasn't best friends with any particular girl, the mushy way they get. The teachers all thought a lot of her, even Miss Eagles. Well, I had to spoil that.

If we'd been like Tot and Mabel, we could have had a lot more time together, I guess. But Helen isn't a liar and I'm not a snake. It wasn't easy, going over to her house, because Mr. and Mrs. Sharon would be polite to each other in front of you and yet there'd be something wrong. And she'd have to be fair to both of them and they were always pulling at her. But we'd look at each other across the table and then it would be all right.

I don't know when it was that we knew we'd get married to each other, some time. We just started talking about it, one day, as if we always had. We were sensible, we knew it couldn't happen right off.

We thought maybe when we were eighteen. That was two years but we knew we had to be educated. You don't get as good a job, if you aren't. Or that's what people say.

We weren't mushy either, like some people. We got to kissing each other good-bye, sometimes, because that's what you do when you're in love. It was cool, the way she kissed you, it was like leaves. But lots of the time we wouldn't even talk about getting married, we'd just play checkers or go over the old Latin, or once in a while go to the movies with the gang. It was really a wonderful winter. I played every game after the first one and she'd sit in the gallery and watch and I'd know she was there. You could see her little green hat or her yellow hair. Those are the class colors, green and gold.

And it's a queer thing, but everybody seemed to be pleased. That's what I can't get over. They liked to see us together. The grown people, I mean. Oh, of course, we got kidded too. And old Mrs. Withers would ask me about "my little sweetheart," in that awful damp voice of hers. But, mostly, they were all right. Even Mother was all right, though she didn't like Mrs. Sharon. I did hear her say to Father, once, "Really, George, how long is this going to last? Sometimes I feel as if I just couldn't stand it."

Then Father chuckled and said to her, "Now, Mary,

last year you were worried about him because he didn't take any interest in girls at all."

"Well," she said, "he still doesn't. Oh, Helen's a nice child—no credit to Eva Sharon—and thank heaven she doesn't giggle. Well, Charles is mature for *his* age too. But he acts so solemn about her. It isn't natural."

"Oh, let Charlie alone," said Father. "The boy's all right. He's just got a one-track mind."

But it wasn't so nice for us after the spring came.

In our part of the state, it comes pretty late, as a rule. But it was early this year. The little kids were out with scooters when usually they'd still be having snowfights and, all of a sudden, the radiators in the classrooms smelt dry. You'd get used to that smell for months—and then, there was a day when you hated it again and everybody kept asking to open the windows. The monitors had a tough time, that first week—they always do when spring starts—but this year it was worse than ever because it came when you didn't expect it.

Usually, basketball's over by the time spring really breaks, but this year it hit us while we still had three games to play. And it certainly played hell with us as a team. After Bladesburg nearly licked us, Mr. Grant called off all practice till the day before the St. Matthew's game. He knew we were stale—and they've been state champions two years. They'd have walked all over us, the way we were going.

The first thing I did was telephone Helen. Because that meant there were six extra afternoons we could have, if she could get rid of her music lessons any way. Well, she said, wasn't it wonderful, her music teacher had a cold? And that seemed just like Fate.

Well, that was a great week and we were so happy. We went to the movies five times and once Mrs. Sharon let us take her little car. She knew I didn't have a driving license but of course I've driven ever since I was thirteen and she said it was all right. She was funny—sometimes she'd be awfully kind and friendly to you and sometimes she'd be like a piece of dry ice. She was that way with Mr. Sharon too. But it was a wonderful ride. We got stuff out of the kitchen—the cook's awfully sold on Helen—and drove way out in the country. And we found an old house, with the windows gone, on top of a hill, and parked the car and took the stuff up to the house and ate it there. There weren't any chairs or tables but we pretended there were.

We pretended it was our house, after we were married. I'll never forget that. She'd even brought paper napkins and paper plates and she set two places on the floor.

"Well, Charles," she said, sitting opposite me, with

her feet tucked under, "I don't suppose you remember the days we were both in school."

"Sure," I said—she was always much quicker pretending things than I was—"I remember them all right. That was before Tot Pickens got to be President." And we both laughed.

"It seems very distant in the past to me—we've been married so long," she said, as if she really believed it. She looked at me.

"Would you mind turning off the radio, dear?" she said. "This modern music always gets on my nerves."

"Have we got a radio?" I said.

"Of course, Chuck."

"With television?"

"Of course, Chuck."

"Gee, I'm glad," I said. I went and turned it off.

"Of course, if you *want* to listen to the late market reports—" she said just like Mrs. Sharon.

"Nope," I said. "The market—uh—closed firm today. Up twenty-six points."

"That's quite a long way up, isn't it?"

"Well, the country's perfectly sound at heart, in spite of this damnfool Congress," I said, like Father.

She lowered her eyes a minute, just like her mother, and pushed away her plate.

"I'm not very hungry tonight," she said. "You won't mind if I go upstairs?"

"Aw, don't be like that," I said. It was too much like her mother.

"I was just seeing if I could," she said. "But I never will, Chuck."

"I'll never tell you you're nervous, either," I said. "I—oh, gosh!"

She grinned and it was all right. "Mr. Ashland and I have never had a serious dispute in our wedded lives," she said—and everybody knows who runs *that* family. "We just talk things over calmly and reach a satisfactory conclusion, usually mine."

"Say, what kind of house have we got?"

"It's a lovely house," she said. "We've got radios in every room and lots of servants. We've got a regular movie projector and a library full of good classics and there's always something in the icebox. I've got a shoe closet."

"A what?"

"A shoe closet. All my shoes are on tipped shelves, like Mother's. And all my dresses are on those padded hangers. And I say to the maid, 'Elsie, Madam will wear the new French model today.' "

"What are all my clothes on?" I said. "Christmas trees?"

"Well," she said. "You've got lots of clothes and dogs. You smell of pipes and the open and something called Harrisburg tweed."

"I do not," I said. "I wish I had a dog. It's a long time since Jack."

"Oh, Chuck, I'm sorry," she said.

"Oh, that's all right," I said. "He was getting old and his ear was always bothering him. But he was a good pooch. Go ahead."

"Well," she said, "of course we give parties—"

"Cut the parties," I said.

"Chuck! They're grand ones!"

"I'm a homebody," I said. "Give me—er—my wife and my little family and—say, how many kids have we got, anyway?"

She counted on her fingers. "Seven."

"Good Lord," I said.

"Well, I always wanted seven. You can make it three, if you like."

"Oh, seven's all right, I suppose," I said. "But don't they get awfully in the way?"

"No," she said. "We have governesses and tutors and send them to boarding school."

"O.K.," I said. "But it's a strain on the old man's pocketbook, just the same."

"Chuck, will you ever talk like that? Chuck, this is when we're rich." Then suddenly, she looked sad. "Oh, Chuck, do you suppose we ever will?" she said.

"Why, sure," I said.

"I wouldn't mind if it was only a dump," she said.

"I could cook for you. I keep asking Hilda how she makes things."

I felt awfully funny. I felt as if I were going to cry.

"We'll do it," I said. "Don't you worry."

"Oh, Chuck, you're a comfort," she said.

I held her for a while. It was like holding something awfully precious. It wasn't mushy or that way. I know what that's like too.

"It takes so long to get old," she said. "I wish I could grow up tomorrow. I wish we both could."

"Don't you worry," I said. "It's going to be all right."

We didn't say much, going back in the car, but we were happy enough. I thought we passed Miss Eagles at the turn. That worried me a little because of the driving license. But, after all, Mrs. Sharon had said we could take the car.

We wanted to go back again, after that, but it was too far to walk and that was the only time we had the car. Mrs. Sharon was awfully nice about it but she said, thinking it over, maybe we'd better wait till I got a license. Well, Father didn't want me to get one till I was seventeen but I thought he might come around. I didn't want to do anything that would get Helen in a jam with her family. That shows how careful I was of her. Or thought I was.

All the same, we decided we'd do something to

celebrate if the team won the St. Matthew's game. We thought it would be fun if we could get a steak and cook supper out somewhere—something like that. Of course we could have done it easily enough with a gang, but we didn't want a gang. We wanted to be alone together, the way we'd been at the house. That was all we wanted. I don't see what's wrong about that. We even took home the paper plates, so as not to litter things up.

Boy, that was a game! We beat them 36-34 and it took an extra period and I thought it would never end. That two-goal lead they had looked as big as the Rocky Mountains all the first half. And they gave me the full school cheer with nine Peters when we tied them up. You don't forget things like that.

Afterwards, Mr. Grant had a kind of spread for the team at his house and a lot of people came in. Kerry had driven down from State to see the game and that made me feel pretty swell. And what made me feel better yet was his taking me aside and saying, "Listen, kid, I don't want you to get the swelled head, but you did a good job. Well, just remember this. Don't let anybody kid you out of going to State. You'll like it up there." And Mr. Grant heard him and laughed and said, "Well, Peters, I'm not proselytizing. But your brother might think about some of the Eastern colleges." It was all like the kind of dream you have when you can do anything. It was wonderful.

Only Helen wasn't there because the only girls were older girls. I'd seen her for a minute, right after the game, and she was fine, but it was only a minute. I wanted to tell her about that big St. Matthew's forward and—oh, everything. Well, you like to talk things over with your girl.

Father and Mother were swell but they had to go on to some big shindy at the country club. And Kerry was going there with Sheila Coe. But Mr. Grant said he'd run me back to the house in his car and he did. He's a great guy. He made jokes about my being the infant phenomenon of basketball, and they were good jokes too. I didn't mind them. But, all the same, when I'd said good night to him and gone into the house, I felt sort of let down.

I knew I'd be tired the next day but I didn't feel sleepy yet. I was too excited. I wanted to talk to somebody. I wandered around downstairs and wondered if Ida was still up. Well, she wasn't, but she'd left half a chocolate cake, covered over, on the kitchen table, and a note on top of it, "Congratulations to Mister Charles Peters." Well, that was awfully nice of her and I ate some. Then I turned the radio on and got the time signal—eleven—and some snappy music. But still I didn't feel like hitting the hay.

So I thought I'd call up Helen and then I thought—

probably she's asleep and Hilda or Mrs. Sharon will answer the phone and be sore. And then I thought— well, anyhow, I could go over and walk around the block and look at her house. I'd get some fresh air out of it, anyway, and it would be a little like seeing her.

So I did—and it was a swell night—cool and a lot of stars—and I felt like a king, walking over. All the lower part of the Sharon house was dark but a window upstairs was lit. I knew it was her window. I went around back of the driveway and whistled once—the whistle we made up. I never expected her to hear.

But she did, and there she was at the window, smiling. She made motions that she'd come down to the side door.

Honestly, it took my breath away when I saw her. She had on a kind of yellow thing over her night clothes and she looked so pretty. Her feet were so pretty in those slippers. You almost expected her to be carrying one of those animals that kids like—she looked young enough. I know I oughtn't to have gone into the house. But we didn't think anything about it—we were just glad to see each other. We hadn't had any sort of chance to talk over the game.

We sat in front of the fire in the living room and she went out to the kitchen and got us cookies and milk. I wasn't really hungry, but it was like that time at the house, eating with her. Mr. and Mrs. Sharon were at the country club, too, so we weren't disturbing them or anything. We turned off the lights because there was plenty of light from the fire and Mr. Sharon's one of those people who can't stand having extra lights burning. Dad's that way about saving string.

It was quiet and lovely and the firelight made shadows on the ceiling. We talked a lot and then we just sat, each of us knowing the other was there. And the room got quieter and quieter and I'd told her about the game and I didn't feel excited or jumpy any more—just rested and happy. And then I knew by her breathing that she was asleep and I put my arm around her for just a minute. Because it was wonderful to hear that quiet breathing and know it was hers. I was going to wake her in a minute. I didn't realize how tired I was myself.

And then we were back in that house in the country and it was our home and we ought to have been happy. But something was wrong because there still wasn't any glass in the windows and a wind kept blowing through them and we tried to shut the doors but they wouldn't shut. It drove Helen distracted and we were both running through the house, trying to shut the doors, and we were cold and afraid. Then the sun rose outside the windows, burning and yellow and so big it covered the sky. And with the sun was

a horrible, weeping voice. It was Mrs. Sharon's saying, "Oh, my God, oh my God."

I didn't know what had happened, for a minute,
when I woke. And then I did and it was awful. Mrs.
Sharon was saying, "Oh, Helen—I trusted you . . ."
and looking as if she were going to faint. And Mr.
Sharon looked at her for a minute and his face was
horrible and he said, "Bred in the bone," and she
looked as if he'd hit her. Then he said to Helen—

I don't want to think of what they said. I don't
want to think of any of the things they said. Mr.
Sharon is a bad man. And she is a bad woman, even
if she is Helen's mother. All the same, I could stand
the things he said better than hers.

I don't want to think of any of it. And it is all spoiled
now. Everything is spoiled. Miss Eagles saw us going
to that house in the country and she said horrible
things. They made Helen sick and she hasn't been
back at school. There isn't any way I can see her. And
if I could, it would be spoiled. We'd be thinking about
the things they said.

I don't know how many of the people know, at
school. But Tot Pickens passed me a note. And, that
afternoon, I caught him behind his house. I'd have
broken his nose if they hadn't pulled me off. I meant
to. Mother cried when she heard about it and Dad
took me into his room and talked to me. He said you

can't lick the whole town. But I will anybody like Tot Pickens. Dad and Mother have been all right. But they say things about Helen and that's almost worse. They're for me because I'm their son. But they don't understand.

I thought I could talk to Kerry but I can't. He was nice but he looked at me such a funny way. I don't know—sort of impressed. It wasn't the way I wanted him to look. But he's been decent. He comes down almost every weekend and we play catch in the yard.

You see, I just go to school and back now. They want me to go with the gang, the way I did, but I can't do that. Not after Tot. Of course my marks are a lot better because I've got more time to study now. But it's lucky I haven't got Miss Eagles though Dad made her apologize. I couldn't recite to her.

I think Mr. Grant knows because he asked me to his house once and we had a conversation. Not about that, though I was terribly afraid he would. He showed me a lot of his old college things and the gold football he wears on his watch chain. He's got a lot of interesting things.

Then we got talking, somehow, about history and things like that and how times had changed. Why, there were kings and queens who got married younger than Helen and me. Only now we lived longer and had a lot more to learn. So it couldn't happen now.

"It's civilization," he said. "And all civilization's against nature. But I suppose we've got to have it. Only sometimes it isn't easy." Well somehow or other, that made me feel less lonely. Before that I'd been feeling that I was the only person on earth who'd ever felt that way.

I'm going to Colorado, this summer, to a ranch, and next year, I'll go East to school. Mr. Grant says he thinks I can make the basketball team, if I work hard enough, though it isn't as big a game in the East as it is with us. Well, I'd like to show them something. It would be some satisfaction. He says not to be too fresh at first, but I won't be that.

It's a boys' school and there aren't even women teachers. And, maybe, afterwards, I could be a professional basketball player or something, where you don't have to see women at all. Kerry says I'll get over that; but I won't. They all sound like Mrs. Sharon to me now, when they laugh.

They're going to send Helen to a convent—I found out that. Maybe they'll let me see her before she goes. But, if we do, it will be all wrong and in front of people and everybody pretending. I sort of wish they don't—though I want to, terribly. When her mother took her upstairs that night—she wasn't the same Helen. She looked at me as if she was afraid of me. And no matter what they do for us now, they can't fix that.

THE
GARDEN PARTY

Katherine Mansfield

nd after all the weather was ideal. They could not have had a more perfect day for a garden party if they had ordered it. Windless, warm, the sky without a cloud. Only the blue was veiled with a haze of light gold, as it is sometimes in early summer. The gardener had been up since dawn, mowing the lawns and sweeping them, until the grass and the dark flat rosettes where the daisy plants had been seemed to shine. As for the roses, you could not help feeling they understood that roses are the only flowers that impress people at garden parties; the only flowers that everybody is certain of knowing. Hundreds, yes, literally hundreds, had come out in a single night; the green bushes bowed down as though they had been visited by archangels.

Breakfast was not yet over before the men came to put up the marquee.

"Where do you want the marquee put, mother?"

"My dear child, it's no use asking me. I'm determined to leave everything to you children this year.

Forget I am your mother. Treat me as an honored guest."

But Meg could not possibly go and supervise the men. She had washed her hair before breakfast, and she sat drinking her coffee in a green turban, with a dark wet curl stamped on each cheek. Jose, the butterfly, always came down in a silk petticoat and a kimono jacket.

"You'll have to go, Laura; you're the artistic one."

Away Laura flew, still holding her piece of bread and butter. It's so delicious to have an excuse for eating out of doors, and besides, she loved having to arrange things; she always felt she could do it so much better than anybody else.

Four men in their shirt-sleeves stood grouped together on the garden path. They carried staves covered with rolls of canvas, and they had big tool bags slung on their backs. They looked impressive. Laura wished now that she had not got the bread and butter, but there was nowhere to put it, and she couldn't possibly throw it away. She blushed and tried to look severe and even a little bit shortsighted as she came up to them.

"Good morning," she said, copying her mother's voice. But that sounded so fearfully affected that she was ashamed, and stammered like a little girl, "Oh— er—have you come—is it about the marquee?"

"That's right, miss," said the tallest of the men, a lanky, freckled fellow, and he shifted his tool bag, knocked back his straw hat and smiled down at her. "That's about it."

His smile was so easy, so friendly that Laura recovered. What nice eyes he had, small, but such a dark blue! And now she looked at the others, they were smiling too. "Cheer up, we won't bite," their smile seemed to say. How very nice workmen were! And what a beautiful morning! She mustn't mention the morning; she must be business-like. The marquee.

"Well, what about the lily lawn? Would that do?"

And she pointed to the lily lawn with the hand that didn't hold the bread and butter. They turned, they stared in the direction. A little fat chap thrust out his underlip, and the tall fellow frowned.

"I don't fancy it," said he. "Not conspicuous enough. You see, with a thing like a marquee," and he turned to Laura in his easy way, "you want to put it somewhere where it'll give you a bang slap in the eye, if you follow me."

Laura's upbringing made her wonder for a moment whether it was quite respectful of a workman to talk to her of bangs slap in the eye. But she did quite follow him.

"A corner of the tennis court," she suggested. "But the band's going to be in one corner."

189

"H'm, going to have a band, are you?" said another of the workmen. He was pale. He had a haggard look as his dark eyes scanned the tennis court. What was he thinking?

"Only a very small band," said Laura gently. Perhaps he wouldn't mind so much if the band was quite small. But the tall fellow interrupted.

"Look here, miss, that's the place. Against those trees. Over there. That'll do fine."

Against the karakas. Then the karaka trees would be hidden. And they were so lovely, with their broad, gleaming leaves, and their clusters of yellow fruit. They were like trees you imagined growing on a desert island, proud, solitary, lifting their leaves and fruits to the sun in a kind of silent splendor. Must they be hidden by a marquee?

They must. Already the men had shouldered their staves and were making for the place. Only the tall fellow was left. He bent down, pinched a sprig of lavender, put his thumb and forefinger to his nose and snuffed up the smell. When Laura saw that gesture she forgot all about the karakas in her wonder at him caring for things like that—caring for the smell of lavender. How many men that she knew would have done such a thing? Oh, how extraordinarily nice workmen were, she thought. Why couldn't she have workmen for friends rather than the silly boys she danced with and who came to Sunday night supper? She would get on much better with men like these.

It's all the fault, she decided, as the tall fellow drew something on the back of an envelope, something that was to be looped up or left to hang, of these absurd class distinctions. Well, for her part, she didn't feel them. Not a bit, not an atom. . . . And now there came the chock-chock of wooden hammers. Some one whistled, some one sang out, "Are you right there, matey?" "Matey!" The friendliness of it, the—the—— Just to prove how happy she was, just to show the tall fellow how at home she felt, and how she despised stupid conventions, Laura took a big bite of her bread and butter as she stared at the drawing. She felt just like a work-girl.

"Laura, Laura, where are you? Telephone, Laura!" a voice cried from the house.

"Coming!" Away she skimmed, over the lawn, up the path, up the steps, across the veranda, and into the porch. In the hall her father and Laurie were brushing their hats ready to go to the office.

"I say, Laura," said Laurie very fast, "you might just give a squiz at my coat before this afternoon. See if it wants pressing."

"I will," said she. Suddenly she couldn't stop herself. She ran at Laurie and gave him a small, quick squeeze. "Oh, I do love parties, don't you?" gasped Laura.

"Ra-ther," said Laurie's warm, boyish voice, and he squeezed his sister too, and gave her a gentle push. "Dash off to the telephone, old girl."

The telephone. "Yes, yes; oh yes. Kitty? Good morning, dear. Come to lunch? Do, dear. Delighted of course. It will only be a very scratch meal—just the sandwich crusts and broken meringue shells and what's left over. Yes, isn't it a perfect morning? Your white? Oh, I certainly should. One moment—hold the line. Mother's calling." And Laura sat back. "What, mother? Can't hear."

Mrs. Sheridan's voice floated down the stairs. "Tell her to wear that sweet hat she had on last Sunday."

"Mother says you're to wear that *sweet* hat you had on last Sunday. Good. One o'clock. Bye-bye."

Laura put back the receiver, flung her arms over her head, took a deep breath, stretched and let them fall. "Huh," she sighed, and the moment after the sigh she sat up quickly. She was still, listening. All the doors in the house seemed to be open. The house was alive with soft, quick steps and running voices. The green baize door that led to the kitchen regions swung open and shut with a muffled thud. And now there came a long, chuckling absurd sound. It was the heavy piano being moved on its stiff castors. But the air! If you stopped to notice, was the air always like this? Little faint winds were playing chase, in at the tops of the windows, out at the doors. And there were two tiny spots of sun, one on the inkpot, one on a silver photograph frame, playing too. Darling little spots. Especially the one on the inkpot lid. It was quite warm. A warm little silver star. She could have kissed it.

The front door bell pealed, and there sounded the rustle of Sadie's print skirt on the stairs. A man's voice murmured; Sadie answered, careless, "I'm sure I don't know. Wait. I'll ask Mrs. Sheridan."

"What is it, Sadie?" Laura came into the hall.

"It's the florist, Miss Laura."

It was, indeed. There, just inside the door, stood a wide, shallow tray full of pots of pink lilies. No other kind. Nothing but lilies—canna lilies, big pink flowers, wide open, radiant, almost frighteningly alive on bright crimson stems.

"O-oh, Sadie!" said Laura, and the sound was like a little moan. She crouched down as if to warm herself at that blaze of lilies; she felt they were in her fingers, on her lips, growing in her breast.

"It's some mistake," she said faintly. "Nobody ever ordered so many. Sadie, go and find mother."

But at that moment Mrs. Sheridan joined them.

"It's quite right," she said calmly. "Yes, I ordered them. Aren't they lovely?" She pressed Laura's arm. "I was passing the shop yesterday, and I saw them in the window. And I suddenly thought for once in my life I shall have enough canna lilies. The garden party will be a good excuse."

"But I thought you said you didn't mean to interfere," said Laura. Sadie had gone. The florist's man was still outside at his van. She put her arm round her mother's neck and gently, very gently, she bit her mother's ear.

"My darling child, you wouldn't like a logical mother, would you? Don't do that. Here's the man."

He carried more lilies still, another whole tray.

"Bank them up, just inside the door, on both sides of the porch, please," said Mrs. Sheridan. "Don't you agree, Laura?"

"Oh, I *do*, mother."

In the drawing-room Meg, Jose and good little Hans had at last succeeded in moving the piano.

"Now, if we put this chesterfield against the wall and move everything out of the room except the chairs, don't you think?"

"Quite."

"Hans, move these tables into the smoking-room, and bring a sweeper to take these marks off the carpet and—one moment, Hans——" Jose loved giving orders to the servants, and they loved obeying her. She always made them feel they were taking part in some drama. "Tell mother and Miss Laura to come here at once."

"Very good, Miss Jose."

She turned to Meg. "I want to hear what the piano sounds like, just in case I'm asked to sing this afternoon. Let's try over 'This Life is Weary.' "

Pom! Ta-ta-ta *Tee*-ta! The piano burst out so passionately that Jose's face changed. She clasped her hands. She looked mournfully and enigmatically at her mother and Laura as they came in.

> This Life is *Wee*-ary,
> A Tear—a Sigh.
> A Love that *Chan*-ges,
>   This Life is *Wee*-ary,
> A Tear—a Sigh.
> A Love that *Chan*-ges,
> And then . . . Good-bye!

But at the word "Good-bye," and although the piano sounded more desperate than ever, her face broke into a brilliant, dreadfully unsympathetic smile.

"Aren't I in good voice, Mummy?" she beamed.

This Life is *Wee*-ary,
Hope comes to Die.
A Dream—a *Wa*-kening.

But now Sadie interrupted them. "What is it, Sadie?"

"If you please, m'm, cook says have you got the flags for the sandwiches?"

"The flags for the sandwiches, Sadie?" echoed Mrs. Sheridan dreamily. And the children knew by her face that she hadn't got them. "Let me see." And she said to Sadie firmly, "Tell cook I'll let her have them in ten minutes."

Sadie went.

"Now, Laura," said her mother quickly. "Come with me into the smoking room. I've got the names somewhere on the back of an envelope. You'll have to write them out for me. Meg, go upstairs this minute and take that wet thing off your head. Jose, run and finish dressing this instant. Do you hear me, children, or shall I have to tell your father when he comes home tonight? And—and, Jose, pacify cook if you do go into the kitchen, will you? I'm terrified of her this morning."

The envelope was found at last behind the dining-room clock, though how it had got there Mrs. Sheridan could not imagine.

"One of you children must have stolen it out of

my bag, because I remember vividly——cream cheese and lemon-curd. Have you done that?"

"Yes."

"Egg and——" Mrs. Sheridan held the envelope away from her. "It looks like mice. It can't be mice, can it?"

"Olive, pet," said Laura, looking over her shoulder.

"Yes, of course, olive. What a horrible combination it sounds. Egg and olive."

They were finished at last, and Laura took them off to the kitchen. She found Jose there pacifying the cook, who did not look at all terrifying.

"I have never seen such exquisite sandwiches," said Jose's rapturous voice. "How many kinds did you say there were, cook? Fifteen?"

"Fifteen, Miss Jose."

"Well, cook, I congratulate you."

Cook swept up crusts with the long sandwich knife, and smiled broadly.

"Godber's has come," announced Sadie, issuing out of the pantry. She had seen the man pass the window.

That meant the cream puffs had come. Godber's were famous for their cream puffs. Nobody ever thought of making them at home.

"Bring them in and put them on the table, my girl," ordered cook.

Sadie brought them in and went back to the door. Of course Laura and Jose were far too grown-up to really care about such things. All the same, they couldn't help agreeing that the puffs looked very attractive. Very. Cook began arranging them, shaking off the extra icing sugar.

"Don't they carry one back to all one's parties?" asked Laura.

"I suppose they do," said practical Jose, who never liked to be carried back. "They look beautifully light and feathery, I must say."

"Have one each, my dears," said cook in her comfortable voice. "Yer ma won't know."

Oh, impossible. Fancy cream puffs so soon after breakfast. The very idea made one shudder. All the same, two minutes later Jose and Laura were licking their fingers with that absorbed inward look that only comes from whipped cream.

"Let's go into the garden, out by the back way," suggested Laura. "I want to see how the men are getting on with the marquee. They're such awfully nice men."

But the back door was blocked by cook, Sadie, Godber's man and Hans.

Something had happened.

"Tuk-tuk-tuk," clucked cook like an agitated hen. Sadie had her hand clapped to her cheek as though she had toothache. Hans's face was screwed up in the effort to understand. Only Godber's man seemed to be enjoying himself; it was his story.

"What's the matter? What happened?"

"There's been a horrible accident," said Cook. "A man killed."

"A man killed! Where? How? When?"

But Godber's man wasn't going to have his story snatched from under his very nose.

"Know those little cottages just below here, miss?" Know them? Of course, she knew them. "Well, there's a young chap living there, name of Scott, a carter. His horse shied at a traction-engine, corner of Hawke Street this morning, and he was thrown out on the back of his head. Killed."

"Dead!" Laura stared at Godber's man.

"Dead when they picked him up," said Godber's man with relish. "They were taking the body home as I come up here." And he said to the cook, "He's left a wife and five little ones."

"Jose, come here." Laura caught hold of her sister's sleeve and dragged her through the kitchen to the other side of the green baize door. There she paused and leaned against it. "Jose!" she said, horrified, "however are we going to stop everything?"

"Stop everything, Laura!" cried Jose in astonishment. "What do you mean?"

"Stop the garden party, of course." Why did Jose pretend?

But Jose was still more amazed. "Stop the garden party? My dear Laura, don't be so absurd. Of course we can't do anything of the kind. Nobody expects us to. Don't be so extravagant."

"But we can't possibly have a garden party with a man dead just outside the front gate."

That really was extravagant, for the little cottages were in a lane to themselves at the very bottom of a steep rise that led up to the house. A broad road ran between. True, they were far too near. They were the greatest possible eyesore, and they had no right to be in that neighbourhood at all. They were little mean dwellings painted a chocolate brown. In the garden patches there was nothing but cabbage stalks, sick hens and tomato cans. The very smoke coming out of their chimneys was poverty-stricken. Little rags and shreds of smoke, so unlike the great silvery plumes that uncurled from the Sheridans' chimneys. Washerwomen lived in the lane and sweeps and a cobbler, and a man whose house front was studded all over with minute bird cages. Children swarmed. When the Sheridans were little they were forbidden to set foot there because of the revolting language and of what they might catch. But since they were grown up, Laura and Laurie on their prowls sometimes walked through. It was disgusting and sordid. They came out with a shudder. But still one must go everywhere; one must see everything. So through they went.

"And just think of what the band would sound like to that poor woman," said Laura.

"Oh, Laura!" Jose began to be seriously annoyed. "If you're going to stop a band playing every time some one has an accident, you'll lead a very strenuous life. I'm every bit as sorry about it as you. I feel just as sympathetic." Her eyes hardened. She looked at her sister just as she used to when they were little and fighting together. "You won't bring a drunken workman back to life by being sentimental," she said softly.

"Drunk! Who said he was drunk?" Laura turned furiously on Jose. She said, just as they had used to say on those occasions, "I'm going straight up to tell mother."

"Do, dear," cooed Jose.

"Mother, can I come into your room?" Laura turned the big glass doorknob.

"Of course, child. Why, what's the matter? What's given you such a color?" And Mrs. Sheridan turned round from her dressing table. She was trying on a new hat.

"Mother, a man's been killed," began Laura.

"*Not* in the garden?" interrupted her mother.

"No, no!"

"Oh, what a fright you gave me!" Mrs. Sheridan sighed with relief, and took off the big hat and held it on her knees.

"But listen, mother," said Laura. Breathless, half-choking, she told the dreadful story. "Of course, we can't have our party, can we?" she pleaded. "The band and everybody arriving. They'd hear us, mother; they're nearly neighbours!"

To Laura's astonishment her mother behaved just like Jose; it was harder to bear because she seemed amused. She refused to take Laura seriously.

"But, my dear child, use your common sense. It's only by accident we've heard of it. If some one had died there normally—and I can't understand how they keep alive in those poky little holes—we should still be having our party, shouldn't we?"

Laura had to say "yes" to that, but she felt it was all wrong. She sat down on her mother's sofa and pinched the cushion frill.

"Mother, isn't it really terribly heartless of us?" she asked.

"Darling!" Mrs. Sheridan got up and came over to her, carrying the hat. Before Laura could stop her she had popped it on. "My child!" said her mother, "the hat is yours. It's made for you. It's much too young for me. I have never seen you look such a picture.

202

Look at yourself!" And she held up her hand mirror.

"But, mother," Laura began again. She couldn't look at herself; she turned aside.

This time Mrs. Sheridan lost patience just as Jose had done.

"You are being very absurd, Laura," she said coldly. "People like that don't expect sacrifices from us. And it's not very sympathetic to spoil everybody's enjoyment as you're doing now."

"I don't understand," said Laura, and she walked quickly out of the room into her own bedroom. There, quite by chance, the first thing she saw was this charming girl in the mirror, in her black hat trimmed with gold daisies, and a long black velvet ribbon. Never had she imagined she could look like that. Is mother right? she thought. And now she hoped her mother was right. Am I being extravagant? Perhaps it was extravagant. Just for a moment she had another glimpse of that poor woman and those little children, and the body being carried into the house. But it all seemed blurred, unreal, like a picture in the newspaper. I'll remember it again after the party's over, she decided. And somehow that seemed quite the best plan. . . .

Lunch was over by half-past one. By half-past two they were all ready for the fray. The green-coated

band had arrived and was established in a corner of
the tennis court.

"My dear!" trilled Kitty Maitland, "aren't they too
like frogs for words? You ought to have arranged
them round the pond with the conductor in the middle
on a leaf."

Laurie arrived and hailed them on his way to dress.
At the sight of him Laura remembered the accident
again. She wanted to tell him. If Laurie agreed with
the others, then it was bound to be all right. And she
followed him into the hall.

"Laurie!"

"Hallo!" He was halfway upstairs, but when he
turned round and saw Laura he suddenly puffed out
his cheeks and goggled his eyes at her. "My word,
Laura! You do look stunning," said Laurie. "What an
absolutely topping hat!"

Laura said faintly "Is it?" and smiled up at Laurie,
and didn't tell him after all.

Soon after that people began coming in streams.
The band struck up; the hired waiters ran from the
house to the marquee. Wherever you looked there
were couples strolling, bending to the flowers, greet-
ing, moving on over the lawn. They were like bright
birds that had alighted in the Sheridans' garden for
this one afternoon, on their way to—where? Ah, what

happiness it is to be with people who all are happy, to press hands, press cheeks, smile into eyes.

"Darling Laura, how well you look!"

"What a becoming hat, child!"

"Laura, you look quite Spanish. I've never seen you look so striking."

And Laura, glowing, answered softly, "Have you had tea? Won't you have an ice? The passion-fruit ices really are rather special." She ran to her father and begged him. "Daddy, darling, can't the band have something to drink?"

And the perfect afternoon slowly ripened, slowly faded, slowly its petals closed.

"Never a more delightful garden party . . ." "The greatest success . . ." "Quite the most . . ."

Laura helped her mother with the good-byes. They stood side by side in the porch till it was all over.

"All over, all over, thank heaven," said Mrs. Sheridan. "Round up the others, Laura. Let's go and have some fresh coffee. I'm exhausted. Yes, it's been very successful. But oh, these parties, these parties! Why will you children insist on giving parties!" And they all of them sat down in the deserted marquee.

"Have a sandwich, Daddy dear. I wrote the flag."

"Thanks." Mr. Sheridan took a bite and the sandwich was gone. He took another. "I suppose you

didn't hear of a beastly accident that happened today?"
he said.

"My dear," said Mrs. Sheridan, holding up her
hand, "we did. It nearly ruined the party. Laura insisted we should put it off."

"Oh, mother!" Laura didn't want to be teased about
it.

"It was a horrible affair all the same," said Mr.
Sheridan. "The chap was married too. Lived just below
in the lane, and leaves a wife and half a dozen kiddies,
so they say."

An awkward little silence fell. Mrs. Sheridan fid-
geted with her cup. Really, it was very tactless of
Father. . . .

Suddenly she looked up. There on the table were
all those sandwiches, cakes, puffs, all uneaten, all going
to be wasted. She had one of her brilliant ideas.

"I know," she said. "Let's make up a basket. Let's
send that poor creature some of this perfectly good
food. At any rate, it will be the greatest treat for the
children. Don't you agree? And she's sure to have
neighbours calling in and so on. What a point to have
it all ready prepared. Laura!" She jumped up. "Get
me the big basket out of the stairs cupboard."

"But, mother, do you really think it's a good idea?"
said Laura.

Again, how curious, she seemed to be different
from them all. To take scraps from their party. Would
the poor woman really like that?

"Of course! What's the matter with you today? An
hour or two ago you were insisting on us being sympathetic, and now——"

Oh, well! Laura ran for the basket. It was filled, it
was heaped by her mother.

"Take it yourself, darling," said she. "Run down
just as you are. No, wait, take the arum lilies too.
People of that class are so impressed by arum lilies."

"The stems will ruin her lace frock," said practical
Jose.

So they would. Just in time. "Only the basket, then.
And, Laura!"—her mother followed her out of the
marquee—"Don't on any account——"

"What, mother?"

No, better not put such ideas into the child's head!
Nothing! Run along."

It was just growing dusky as Laura shut their garden
gates. A big dog ran by like a shadow. The road
gleamed white, and down below in the hollow the
little cottages were deep in shade. How quiet it seemed
after the afternoon. Here she was going down the hill
to somewhere where a man lay dead, and she couldn't
realize it. Why couldn't she? She stopped a minute.

And it seemed to her that kisses, voices, tinkling spoons, laughter, the smell of crushed grass were somehow inside her. She had no room for anything else. How strange! She looked up at the pale sky, and all she thought was, "Yes, it was the most successful party."

Now the broad road was crossed. The lane began, smoky and dark. Women in shawls and men's tweed caps hurried by. Men hung over the palings; the children played in the doorways. A low hum came from the mean little cottages. In some of them there was a flicker of light, and a shadow, crab-like, moved across the window. Laura bent her head and hurried on. She wished now she had put on a coat. How her frock shone! And the big hat with the velvet streamer—if only it was another hat! Were the people looking at her? They must be. It was a mistake to have come; she knew all along it was a mistake. Should she go back even now?

No, too late. This was the house. It must be. A dark knot of people stood outside. Beside the gate an old, old woman with a crutch sat in a chair, watching. She had her feet on a newspaper. The voices stopped as Laura drew near. The group parted. It was as though she was expected, as though they had known she was coming here.

Laura was terribly nervous. Tossing the velvet ribbon over her shoulder, she said to a woman standing by, "Is this Mrs. Scott's house?" and the woman, smiling queerly, said, "It is, my lass."

Oh, to be away from this! She actually said, "Help me, God," as she walked up the tiny path and knocked. To be away from those staring eyes, or to be covered up in anything, one of those women's shawls, even. I'll just leave the basket and go, she decided. I shan't even wait for it to be emptied.

Then the door opened. A little woman in black showed in the gloom.

Laura said, "Are you Mrs. Scott?" But to her horror the woman answered, "Walk in please, miss," and she was shut in the passage.

"No," said Laura, "I don't want to come in. I only want to leave this basket. Mother sent——"

The little woman in the gloomy passage seemed not to have heard her. "Step this way, please, miss," she said in an oily voice, and Laura followed her.

She found herself in a wretched little low kitchen, lighted by a smoky lamp. There was a woman sitting before the fire.

"Em," said the little creature who had let her in. "Em! It's a young lady." She turned to Laura. She said meaningly, "I'm 'er sister, Miss. You'll excuse 'er, won't you?"

"Oh, but of course!" said Laura. "Please, please don't disturb her. I—I only want to leave——"

But at that moment the woman at the fire turned round. Her face, puffed up, red, with swollen eyes and swollen lips, looked terrible. She seemed as though she couldn't understand why Laura was there. What did it mean? Why was this stranger standing in the kitchen with a basket? What was it all about? And the poor face puckered up again.

"All right, my dear," said the other. "I'll thenk the young lady."

And again she began, "You'll excuse her, miss, I'm sure," and her face, swollen too, tried an oily smile.

Laura only wanted to get out, to get away. She was back in the passage. The door opened. She walked straight through into the bedroom, where the dead man was lying.

"You'd like a look at 'im, wouldn't you?" said Em's sister, and she brushed past Laura over to the bed. "Don't be afraid, my lass,—" and now her voice sounded fond and sly, and fondly she drew down the sheet—" 'e looks a picture. There's nothing to show. Come along, my dear."

Laura came.

There lay a young man, fast asleep—sleeping so soundly, so deeply, that he was far, far away from them both. Oh, so remote, so peaceful. He was dreaming. Never wake him up again. His head was sunk in the pillow, his eyes were closed; they were blind under the closed eyelids. He was given up to his dream. What did garden parties and baskets and lace frocks matter to him? He was far from all those things. He was wonderful, beautiful. While they were laughing and while the band was playing, this marvel had come to the lane. Happy . . . happy. . . . All is well, said that sleeping face. This is just as it should be. I am content.

But all the same you had to cry, and she couldn't go out of the room without saying something to him. Laura gave a loud childish sob.

"Forgive my hat," she said.

And this time she didn't wait for Em's sister. She found her way out of the door, down the path, past all those dark people. At the corner of the lane she met Laurie.

He stepped out of the shadow. "Is that you, Laura?"

"Yes."

"Mother was getting anxious. Was it all right?"

"Yes, quite. Oh, Laurie!" She took his arm, she pressed up against him.

"I say, you're not crying, are you?" asked her brother.

Laura shook her head. She was.

Laurie put his arm round her shoulder. "Don't cry," he said in his warm, loving voice. "Was it awful?"

"No," sobbed Laura. "It was simply marvelous. But, Laurie——" She stopped, she looked at her brother. "Isn't life," she stammered, "isn't life——" But what life was she couldn't explain. No matter. He quite understood.

"*Isn't* it, darling?" said Laurie.